"Why are you afraid of me, Maxie," he asked.

It was the sort of challenge she could never resist.

"I'm not afraid of the devil," she said.

"Every time I kiss you, you run like hell. I know it's not displeasure, because you kiss me back." She opened her mouth to argue, but he didn't give her time. "That leaves only one alternative: fear."

Unconsciously, she put the cool glass of lemonade to the flushed skin of her neck.

"Don't you dare slide that glass down your blouse. I'm only human, you know."

"Is that why you back me into every piece of furniture you can find, every time you see me?"

"I know it's not a gentlemanly thing to do. It's hardly even civil." He grinned. "But what can I say, Maxie? You're irresistible. . . ."

WHAT ARE *LOVESWEPT* ROMANCES?

They are stories of true romance and touching emotion. We believe those two very important ingredients are constants in our highly sensual and very believable stories in the LOVE-SWEPT line. Our goal is to give you, the reader, stories of consistently high quality that may sometimes make you laugh, sometimes make you cry, but are always fresh and creative and contain many delightful surprises within their pages.

Most romance fans read an enormous number of books. Those they truly love, they keep. Others may be traded with friends and soon forgotten. We hope that each LOVESWEPT romance will be a treasure—a "keeper." We will always try to publish

LOVE STORIES YOU'LL NEVER FORGET
BY AUTHORS YOU'LL ALWAYS REMEMBER

The Editors

ANGELS
ON
ZEBRAS

PEGGY WEBB

BANTAM BOOKS
NEW YORK · TORONTO · LONDON · SYDNEY · AUCKLAND

ANGELS ON ZEBRAS

A Bantam Book / January 1998

ISBN 0-553-44654-1

Published simultaneously in the United States and Canada

*Bantam Books are published by Bantam Books, a division of Bantam Dou-
bleday Dell Publishing Group, Inc. Its trademark, consisting of the words
"Bantam Books" and the portrayal of a rooster, is Registered in U.S.
Patent and Trademark Office and in other countries. Marca Registrada.
Bantam Books, 1540 Broadway, New York, New York 10036.*

PRINTED IN THE UNITED STATES OF AMERICA

OPM   10 9 8 7 6 5 4 3 2 1

Once more for Cecilia,
who first saw angels on zebras,
and for Tom, who understands magic

ONE

"Why can't we have real zebras?"

Joseph cringed at the question, but everybody else in the barbershop seemed to think it was the most amusing thing since Randall, the owner, had announced to his regular customers that he'd had nothing for breakfast except fruit of the looms.

"Why can't she have zebras?" Randall asked, nudging the Wednesday regular in the chair next to Joseph's.

The Wednesday regular lifted the hot towel off his face and grinned like the Cheshire cat. "Yeah, Joseph. Why can't she? It seems a pretty little thing like her ought to be able to have anything she wants."

"Thanks, fellas," Maxie said, grinning at her supporters. Every man in the shop swooned.

Every man except Joseph. Her charm was fatal. He supposed that's why she was called Magic Maxie. But he had no intention of falling victim . . . again.

Godchild or no godchild.

The next time he saw his brother he was going to kill him. If Crash hadn't come up with the harebrained scheme of naming his wife's sister as godmother, Joseph would be sitting in the barber's chair getting a nice shave and haircut and talking politics instead of being bombarded with crazy ideas by Maxie Corban. He would be planning to get in his Lincoln and take a sedate drive to his law office instead of fielding ridiculous ideas for the christening party with Crash's scatterbrained sister-in-law.

"We can't have real zebras because the whole idea is absurd," he said.

"Why?" Maxie asked.

"Yeah," Randall chimed in, snipping in earnest around Joseph's ear. "That's what I'd like to know."

"You stay out of this, Randall."

"You know the rules, Joe. Everything said in this barbershop is my business." Randall winked at Maxie. "The lady's waiting for an answer."

If he'd been in a courtroom, Joseph could have snapped out a brilliant reply in two seconds flat. But darned if he didn't have to ponder before he could come up with a response to Maxie.

Of course, it wasn't every day he carried on a conversation with a woman who looked like a cross between a sugarplum fairy and a naughty child. Her hands moved when she talked, and so did her hair, a mop of red curls caught high on her head by a bright orange ribbon. As if that color combination weren't enough to shock, she was wearing mismatched shoes, one pink and one red. Her miniskirt was some fantastic shade of pink that he was certain glowed in the dark, and her raw silk jacket was neon blue.

He wondered if she dressed like that every day or only on special occasions. For a man who had spent the last nine months avoiding her company, it was a foolish thing to wonder.

In fact, he hadn't done much better himself. When Crash had called and yelled into the phone, "You're an uncle," Joseph had actually gone out of the house without shaving. That's why he was at the barbershop now. He'd never gone to work looking scruffy, and he didn't intend to start.

The heat rose in his face when Maxie tipped her head to one side and widened her eyes at him. His resolve weakened.

"The zebras," she prompted.

"Why zebras?" It was a good stalling tactic, using a question to field a question.

"Because they're lively and fun, and sometimes angels ride them."

Was he hearing things? Joseph had the kind of steel-trap mind that never missed a word, not even a single nuance. Maybe it was the snipping of the scissors that distracted him. It surely couldn't be the enticing curve of Maxie's legs, though she made crossing them an art.

"I beg your pardon?" He sounded like a bullfrog in heat. Studiously avoiding looking at her legs, he cleared his throat and resisted the impulse to run his finger around his collar to release the heat. "Did you say *angels on zebras*?"

"Yes. Sometimes. I use them in the nurseries. Especially with boys."

Joseph actually glanced around to see if he'd fallen down the rabbit hole and was conversing with Alice. After all, Maxie did have a ribbon in her hair. Not many women past the age of sixteen wore colored ribbons in their hair.

Certainly not Susan. His fiancée wouldn't be caught dead with an ornament of any kind in her hair, let alone a ribbon. That was one thing that made her so perfect for Joseph: her bone-deep conservatism. She had other sterling qualities, of course, but he was hard-pressed to think of them right now.

He could barely remember his own name, for the bewitching Maxie had just run her tongue over her bottom lip.

"What nurseries?" He felt disoriented, as if he'd landed on another planet in another body, one bent on betraying him. He controlled the rising tide of heat with an iron will. "What boys?"

"Oh, not real ones. Wallpaper ones."

"Wallpaper boys?" Was there something Crash hadn't told him about Maxie? For instance, that she was a little bit batty?

Her laughter was full and deep-throated, surprising in such a small woman, and altogether enchanting. Luckily he wasn't the kind of man who fell victim to enchantment.

"The boys are real, of course. The zebras are not.

They're painted on the wallpaper I sometimes use when I decorate nurseries for my clients."

"I see."

Joseph had completely forgotten that she was an interior designer. In her company, it was easy to forget a lot of things.

Her shop was called Magic Maxie's, an appropriate name considering that she was given to flights of fancy even in such mundane surroundings as Randall's Barber Shop and Emporium, the emporium part due to a rack of paperback books the owner sold at a discount and a shelf of very fine cigars he stocked on all major holidays.

Fortunately, Randall considered the Ides of March a major holiday. When Joseph got back to his office he would pass out cigars in honor of being a godfather.

That is, *if* he ever got back. At the rate Maxie was going, he might be there until next Wednesday, still trying to catch the drift of her conversation.

"My favorite is the border with the angels riding circus animals," she said. "It's so fanciful and marvelous." She tipped her head and shot a brilliant smile in his direction. "I think every child should be exposed to something marvelous, don't you?"

If it hadn't been for her smile, he could readily have disagreed. Only a monster would contradict her and risk snuffing out that smile.

"I never gave it any thought, but yes, I suppose a marvel every now and then might be appropriate."

He couldn't think of a single marvelous thing he'd seen or done in the last fifteen years. Or maybe ever.

His brother, Crash, was the fanciful one. Joseph had always been focused and reliable, with his feet firmly planted on the ground . . . with one notable exception.

He pushed the memory to the back of his mind.

"Great," Maxie said, whipping a small notepad out of her hot pink shoulder bag. What else did he expect? She dashed off a note. "I'm glad you agree."

"Now wait a minute. I haven't agreed to anything." Her smile made him think of angels with crooked halos and bedraggled wings. "What did you write in that notebook?"

"A reminder to call Quitman this afternoon . . . about the zebras."

He leaped from his chair as if she'd set off rockets under his coattail.

"I will not have zebras at my nephew's christening party. Not only is it undignified, but it has all the makings of a disaster."

He knew he was towering over her, but he didn't care. He was not going to be persuaded to do something foolish simply because she looked tiny and fragile staring up at him with her big blue eyes. Maxie Corban was anything but fragile.

"Don't blame me if you have a gap in your hair," Randall said. "Party pooper."

"Thank you, Randall." Maxie beamed at him. "I couldn't have said it better myself."

Joseph figured the best thing to do was ignore them, though ignoring Maxie was about as easy as ignoring a stick of dynamite with a lit fuse. She marched up behind him as he shrugged into his navy blazer.

"How about a nice cuddly lamb or two? We could get those at Crash and B. J.'s farm."

"No live animals. End of discussion."

He headed for the door, deliberately trying to outdistance her. But she matched him stride for stride. She had long legs for a small woman, long, shapely legs. She put him in mind of that old Betty Grable pinup his granddaddy Beauregard had tacked in his barracks during World War II.

"How can it be the end of the discussion? We've agreed on absolutely nothing. We haven't even *begun.*"

All activity in the shop ceased as Maxie walked by. Correct that, Joe thought. Maxie didn't walk. She marched, she strutted, she paraded.

"I'm going to the office."

He strode toward his car. Maxie had parked beside him, a fiery red Volkswagen Beetle with a broad white stripe and a dented top. Next to his big black Lincoln, her car looked like a peppermint somebody had stepped on.

"I'll come with you."

"*No.*"

He could picture it, Maxie sweeping through his office, eyebrows lifting, tongues wagging. He glanced down at her. The top of her head barely came to his shoulder, and in the bright sun her hair blazed, poppies streaked with gold.

Joseph moderated his tone. "I'm going to be late for my ten o'clock appointment."

"The christening party is only six weeks away."

"That gives us plenty of time."

"Not if future meetings go the way this one did. We didn't agree on a single thing today."

"That's my fault. I should never have agreed to talk about it today. Randall's barbershop is not an appropriate setting for a business meeting."

"A business meeting?" Maxie looked as if she'd discovered a bug in her soup. "This is a *party* we're talking about. For *my* nephew."

"He's mine too."

"Well, you certainly don't act like it. For all the enthusiasm you show, he might as well be one of those criminals you defend."

"I'm a corporate attorney."

"That's what I said." Her grin was as pert as her stance.

A man could get sidetracked by the way she looked standing in the sun, eyes shooting fire and every part of her body thrust forward and wired for battle. Fortunately, he was not that kind of man. His life was mapped out right down to the silver pattern he used to eat his spaghetti every Wednesday night. Maxie Corban was merely a necessary and temporary diversion.

"In spite of what you might think, I'm deeply concerned about this party and have every desire that it proceed as smoothly as possible." He glanced at his watch. Fifteen minutes late. A quarter of a billable hour. "When I get to the office I'll have my secretary call your secretary to set up an appointment. . . . You do have a secretary, don't you?"

"I have Claude."

She had as many different kinds of smiles as she did moods. The one she gave him made her as mysterious and intriguing as the Mona Lisa.

All the way to the office he wondered who Claude was . . . and what he did for Maxie Corban besides the typing.

"You mean he nixed *every* idea you presented?" Claude pressed his hands to his cheeks in horror.

"Everything," Maxie said.

"Well, dear, I hope you gave him a piece of your mind."

"I don't have any to spare, Claude."

"Tsk, tsk. You are *the* most brilliant and talented person in Tupelo. With the possible exception of myself."

Claude went to the kitchenette and made two cups of hot tea.

Maxie's shop was in a small loft over an antiques shop on Main Street. Bright paintings and prints covered the walls, a sectional sofa upholstered in vivid pink faced the wide sweep of French windows, and a large oak drafting table strewn with colorful fabric swatches divided the main workroom from the kitchenette.

Claude handed her a cup of tea. "I put two lumps of sugar in yours. You need the extra energy after dealing with that *lump*."

Claude talked as if he were onstage, punctuating

his speech with dramatic gestures and emphatic enunciation.

"He's not a lump."

"Well, darling, he's certainly not Mr. Perfect."

Maxie was not above dramatics herself. Heaving a sigh worthy of the divas of the silver screen, she sank onto the sofa, holding her tea carefully between cupped hands.

"Once upon a time I thought so." She sighed once more. "Did I ever tell you about the first time we met?"

"It's been a while. . . . Refresh me on the details, darling."

"It was when B. J. decided to have a baby . . ." she began.

It had been nine months, almost to the day, Maxie remembered. She had gone to a banquet for Tupelo's elite to help her sister find the perfect father, and there he was, Joseph Patrick Beauregard, Mr. Right. Mr. Perfect. Mr. Dreamboat.

B. J. didn't think so, of course. She only had eyes for his brother, but Maxie was smitten, snowed, dazzled, enchanted. Until . . .

"There we were," she said, concluding her story, "Mr. Dreamboat and I, sitting side by side in the moonlight at B. J.'s first social gathering after her marriage, not saying a word to each other for two solid hours."

"Not a single *word*?" Claude clapped his hands over his cheeks, aghast for the hundredth time. Maxie took comfort in the familiar.

"Well, I tried at first, but I gave up after he turned two shades of pale when I introduced the subject of the mating habits of the praying mantis . . . you know, the female eats the male after they mate. Crash and B. J. thought it was funny, but Joseph didn't even crack a smile."

Not only that, but she'd later overheard him in the foyer telling Crash his sister-in-law was highly inappropriate.

Inappropriate for what, she'd like to know. But she would never ask. Not in a million years.

Especially after what had happened that night in B. J.'s guest bedroom.

"And that's it?" Claude leaned forward, his teacup delicately balanced on his knees. "He's avoided you because of praying mantises?"

"*I've* avoided him."

There were some things she couldn't tell even her best friend.

"Of course, darling. That's the way it ought to be."

Maxie jumped up and paced the loft, then stood at the window. Across the street Kathy pulled up the shades in the art gallery, readying the historic bank building for the small flurry of art lovers who would come inside on their lunch hours.

Behind her the phone rang.

"Hello," Claude said. Then, "Just a minute, I'll see if she's in." He covered the receiver with his hand. "Are you in?"

"Who is it?"

"Joseph Patrick Beauregard."

Chills went all over Maxie. "Not his secretary?"

"The man himself."

"Tell him . . . I'm not in."

"She's not in. Can I take a message?"

Maxie tensed, waiting. Only after she heard the click of the receiver did she relax.

"He wants to see you after-hours tomorrow, to discuss the baby's party."

"What time?"

"Around six. I told him I'd check with you and let him know."

She felt as if she were on a carousel, giddy and dizzy, spinning round and round with no way off.

"Call him back in about an hour and say . . ."

What? Maxie Corban doesn't want to see you because she's a coward? Because she can't forget a hot summer night nearly a year ago?

". . . say I'll be there."

"Maxie . . . Are you all right, dear? You look as if you've seen a ghost."

"I have, practically."

"It's that man, isn't it? Good grief, I wouldn't care a flitter what he thought about my conversational skills."

"That's not all there is to it, Claude."

"I knew it." Claude sat down and patted the sofa cushion beside him. "Tell me all about it. You know you can trust me with your deepest, darkest secret."

Maxie kicked off her shoes and tucked her feet under her.

"The truth is, he still rings my chimes."

"Then I wouldn't let something as silly as praying mantises stop me from a little ting-a-ling."

"It's not that. It's B. J."

"Your *sister*? I knew she was straitlaced, but I didn't know she was a prude."

"It's nothing she's said or done, it's me. You know my track record with men. Every man I get involved with ends up in a wilderness somewhere contemplating his navel. My sister loves her brother-in-law. She'd die if I was the cause of his ruination. Somebody else might ruin Joseph Patrick Beauregard, but it won't be me."

"Do you want my advice, or do you want me just to listen?"

"Just listen."

"That's what I thought." Claude sipped his tea. "It's hard, though. I do love meddling in other people's affairs. Especially yours. They're so exciting."

Claude could always make her laugh. She guessed that was one of the reasons they were such good friends.

"Can you come by the house tonight? I'm going to watch *I Love Lucy* reruns and eat tons of popcorn with butter."

"Anything for Magic Maxie."

"Thanks, Claude. If there's anything I can do for you, just let me know."

"There is one thing."

"Name it."

"Take my advice. . . . Now, don't get that look.

This is not about you-know-who, it's about the christening party. Just plan the thing yourself and let that
odious man stew in his own juices."

"I'm tempted."

"Then why don't you do it?"

"I can't. B. J. named both of us as godparents. My
sister is counting on me."

TWO

There was no way he could get around it. His brother was counting on him.

Still gripping the phone, Joseph listened to the click of the receiver.

"So, Joseph Patrick Beauregard," he muttered. "What other excuses do you have for being a fool?"

He should have had one of his secretaries make the call. That's what he paid them for, to keep him from having to deal with details.

But there was always the off chance that Maxie would answer her own phone.

A vivid memory flashed through his mind, Maxie with red lips pressed close to the receiver, her voice soft and seductive . . .

His instant response to the image took Joseph by surprise, and he sat gripping the phone, trying to get himself under control.

"Dammit."

He slammed down the phone and stalked to the window. That woman was a sorceress. He never said a cuss word and he never wasted time dawdling at his window.

It was a blessing Maxie Corban hadn't answered her own phone. He shuddered to think of the state she might have put him in. From her, even a simple hello was erotic.

He stood at his window hoping the peaceful scene would act as a balm on his aroused body and agitated mind.

His law office was a converted Victorian house on Broadway, which was known informally around town as Lawyers' Row, a charming old house set in a yard full of old-fashioned shrubs and flowers. The forsythia was in bloom. And the crab apple. Azalea bushes were full of buds and would soon burst into a glorious display of white and pink and red blossoms.

But nothing could distract him. His mind worried at the problem the way a bee buzzed around the throat of a spring blossom.

The smart thing to do was let Jenny or Pam make all the arrangements, let one of them plan the party with Maxie. Both would do it willingly, and he could wash his hands of the whole deal.

Then he wouldn't have to talk to Maxie again, wouldn't have to see her until the christening.

But, of course, he wouldn't. He'd always been there for his brother, and he would do this, too, even if it caused him ulcers and temporary insanity.

Turning quickly from the garden view, he strode to his desk and buzzed for Jenny.

"Call Susan and tell her I'll pick her up at eight."

She would be the perfect distraction, he decided, and then was ashamed of himself for thinking of his fiancée as an antidote.

He rang the doorbell only once. Susan was always punctual.

"Hello, darling." She kissed him lightly on the lips, then turned immediately to get her purse off the hall table.

He wondered how she would react if he ran his hands under her sweater then bent her over that table for a quickie. She would probably think he'd gone mad.

On the other hand, it was just the sort of thing Maxie would love.

Guilt slashed him.

"You look lovely tonight," he said.

"Thank you. Your house, as usual?"

"Yes. My house as usual."

He thrived on routine. Didn't he?

"Great. I've been looking forward to your spaghetti all day . . . and seeing you, of course."

Today he'd clearly been an afterthought to Susan, but he supposed that was exactly what he deserved. She hadn't been at the forefront of his mind, either.

Maxie's lips were lush and ripe, and when she said hello

she drew out the last syllable so that her lips formed a perfect circle.

Joseph's passion stirred, and he felt guilty that Susan wasn't the cause.

She threaded her arm through his, and as they walked to the car he wondered what his fiancée would do if he proposed something different, pizza at Vanelli's or fish at Malone's or even a barbecue at Johnny's Drive In.

She was wearing a gray wool skirt and cashmere sweater with pearls and heels. He couldn't imagine her kicked back in his Lincoln with barbecue sauce running down her chin.

On the other hand, Maxie . . .

"Did you say something, Joseph?"

"Just clearing my throat."

If he could get through the christening, everything would be all right. Six weeks to go. Six weeks of contact with the woman who was more lethal than a stiletto in the heart.

In the car Susan's perfume settled over him like a pall. It was something exotic and spicy with a sticky sweet note that made Joseph think of funerals.

He pressed a button on the automatic control panel, then leaned his head out the window and took several deep, fortifying breaths.

"Joseph? Are you all right?"

Good Lord. He even felt guilty breathing.

"I'm okay."

"Are you sure? You haven't seemed yourself this evening."

"I'm fine." He backed out of her driveway. "Is that a new perfume you're wearing?"

"Don't be silly. I *never* change perfumes. Find a fragrance you like and stick to it. That's my motto." She ran her finger along the back of his neck. "Same as men. Find one you like and stick to him."

Joseph had a sudden vision of Susan with an enormous brush slathering glue all over him then attaching herself like a third arm or leg. Quickly he shook off the image. He was being unfair to Susan. Not only was she a brilliant psychiatrist, but she was a well-bred woman, lovely, courteous, and kind.

All the way home he congratulated himself on having had the good sense to propose to her.

His house was a Tudor mansion in the old section of Tupelo. Every time he entered Highland Circle he felt a sense of order. The lots were perfectly sized so that neighboring houses were close enough to feel friendly but not so close as to be intrusive. The trees were old and stately, the lawns immaculate, the houses well kept.

He made a ritual of hanging his jacket in the hall closet, of checking his mail on the hall table where his housekeeper Hazel left it, of turning on the gas fire in the library, where his antique lamps glowed against the burgundy leather sofa. By the time he finished his routine, Susan was already in *her* wing chair, reading the financial section of the *Wall Street Journal.*

Seized by a sudden mad impulse, he bent over the back of her chair and traced her earlobe with his tongue.

"Joseph . . . that tickles." Her eyes never left the newspaper.

"That's all? It tickles?" Wounded pride was speaking.

Susan put down the paper. "Darling, we always wait until after dinner for that sort of thing."

And so they did. It was an orderly routine that fit perfectly into his carefully planned life.

"Of course, we can reverse the order of things if you can't wait," she said.

He could certainly wait. Temporary insanity had prompted him, not passion. He was grateful to her for restoring his sanity.

"No, everything's fine, darling. You just sit there and finish reading while I get dinner."

As he entered his orderly kitchen, Joseph's world righted itself, and he hummed as he dished up two china plates of spaghetti. It was an old family recipe, and although Hazel had been the one to make it, Susan still called it his spaghetti.

The evening progressed with a comforting predictability that almost wiped Maxie from his mind. Soon he would take Susan upstairs to his bed, where the familiar routine of nice simple sex would erase the last vestige of the titian-haired enchantress.

He hoped.

"Darling, do you mind if I check my messages before we go upstairs? One of my patients was verging on hysteria today."

"Of course not, Susan. Your patient's lucky to have a doctor like you. And so am I."

He kissed her on the lips. Hard. Hoping for the kind of skyrockets he'd felt that afternoon in his office while he'd sat holding the telephone.

"Joseph!" She pushed playfully at him. "What's gotten into you?"

"You don't like it?"

"Not yet, darling. After I make this call we'll try it again."

They didn't.

Susan ended up meeting her hysterical patient at the hospital, and Joseph ended up driving around the city without purpose. Something he never did.

Suddenly he found himself on the country road that led to his brother's farm.

"Joseph! What brings you here?"

"Impulse."

Crash hooted with laughter. "There may be hope for you yet." He led Joseph inside. "I'm headed to the hospital to see B. J. and baby Joe. Want to come?"

"I won't intrude on your privacy. You go ahead. I'll just sit here for a while."

"Make yourself at home. And don't leave till I get back. I want to hear all about your meeting with Maxie." Crash laughed. "I can tell by the look on your face it's going to be quite a story."

Suddenly Joseph knew why he had come to his brother's house: It was the only connection he had to a red-haired sprite who for one summer night had driven him mad—wonderfully, wickedly, deliciously mad.

He had come on a pilgrimage. He had to see for himself if the place still held the magic.

"I'll be here," he said.

He couldn't leave, even if he wanted to, for already the room down the hall was beckoning him.

As his brother's car pulled out of the driveway, Joseph stood in the middle of the guest bedroom surveying his surroundings. Intent on re-creating the exact setting of nine months earlier, he'd left all the lights off except the bedside lamp. A soft pool of light fell across the ivory comforter in precisely the spot where she had been, red hair gleaming, hips in a sexy mound, breasts ripe and lush with nipples as pink and tight as rosebuds.

Joseph heard a harsh, guttural sound, and it was a moment before he knew it came from him. It was half desire, half denial. But there was no denying the rush of heat, the instantaneous arousal, the quickened pulse.

He made himself look away, forced himself to catalogue the antique dressing table, the carved mantel with photographs of three generations of Beauregards framed in silver, the gas logs, unlit, the French doors with heavy damask draperies.

Joseph closed the drapes. He wanted everything to be exactly as it had been that hot summer night.

He was tempted to linger in the bedroom where she had been, tempted to caress the pillow where her hair had fanned out like flame, tempted to run his hands over the coverlet where her legs had been so wantonly spread.

Joseph balled his hands into fists and walked stoically toward the connecting door. Inside the bathroom he turned on the light. Twelve naked bulbs flashed against the white tiles, a stark and startling light that illuminated the lines fanning out from his eyes, the streak of gray in his dark hair, the stress etched around his mouth.

Joe propped himself on the sink and leaned in close.

"You look like hell," he said to his image.

He loosened his tie, then splashed his face with cold water. The water did nothing to cool his ardor. Memories are often stronger than will, and they poured over him, through him, around him, until he was leaning heavily against the sink, gripping the cold porcelain as if he could rid himself of their power by sheer force.

His mind swirled, and he was cast back in time, back to the soft summer night when he'd stood in that very spot, stripped of his clothes, stripped of his pride, stripped of reason, stripped of everything except passion.

He closed his eyes, and echoes of her voice drifted through the doorway, the throaty, sexy voice of a woman bent on seduction. . . .

THREE

"I want you to lick me all over, starting with my toes."

The female voice was an intimate purr, coming through the slightly open door of the adjoining room.

Riveted, Joseph had stood at the edge of the sink, his swim trunks dripping water on the tiles, his hands hovering over the faucets, his skin turning hot. He'd thought he was alone in the house.

"Rake your hot tongue over my instep . . . move slowly upward, slowly, slow . . . ly to the back of my leg, behind my knee . . . ohhh, that feels gooood. . . ."

Desire slammed Joseph so hard he had to clamp his lower lip between his teeth to keep from groaning. Outside the bathroom window he could hear the sounds of Crash's laughter mingled with the musical cadences of his brother's new bride as they fired up the grill.

Joseph had arrived early for the party, intent on

doing a few laps in the pool before dinner. All the guests would swim later in the evening, but Joe preferred having the pool all to himself. He was as serious about swimming as he was about law. No horsing around for him, just serious laps designed to increase endurance.

"Do you feel how hot my skin is? It's on fire. Lick it . . . put out the flames."

A big drop of moisture fell into the sink, and Joe didn't know whether it was water or sweat. He glanced at the door he'd come through, judging whether he could ease back into the bathroom and out into the hall without making any noise.

The voice seduced, carrying through the crack in the doorway as clearly as if Joe were in the room. There was no answering male voice, not even a murmur. The woman was alone.

"Ohhh, I'm so hot tonight. Slick and wet and hot. Feel that heat with your tongue."

Caught up in her erotic images, Joe abandoned all thought of trying for escape and gave himself over to the spell cast by the mystery woman in the adjoining bedroom.

"Find the spot . . . ohhhh, that's it. Are you hard yet?"

That was an understatement. Joe was about to explode.

Her voice washed over him, rich, seductive, full of erotic promise. His hand eased to the front of his swim trunks.

"I want you . . . now . . . come to me . . .

come in out of the cold . . . inside where it's nice and soft and warm."

In his mind Joe followed her instructions. Pure unadulterated pleasure jolted through him. Everything in the bathroom spun away, and Joe was inside the bedroom, inside the woman whose voice seduced him, enchanted him, bewitched him.

What did she look like? This temptress with a voice of silk and fire. This erotic enchantress. This seductress with the delightfully naughty twist of mind.

The door was open a crack. Did he dare risk a peek?

His mind reeling, his body achingly aroused, Joe craned his neck toward the crack in the door. A wisp of bright pink lay on the floor, a very small bikini swimsuit with hardly enough material for a handkerchief.

"Fool," he told himself. "Look away."

But he couldn't. He saw feet, small, dainty feet with high insteps and toenails painted an outrageous purple. His gaze moved upward. There were legs, long, shapely, suntanned legs.

"Ohhh," she said. "I want you so much. . . ."

Her fingernails were painted the same as her toes, the purple vivid against her skin as her hands moved.

Her body was irresistible, impossibly perfect. A platoon of armed Martians couldn't have kept Joe from wanting to see more.

He took one step toward the door . . . then another.

"You are sooo hard, sooo big," she whispered.

How did she know? Now that he was standing in the crack of the door, Joe couldn't move.

Shamelessly he took in the full length of her, spread across the bed, neck arched, hair fanning across the pillow like flame, red lips lush and pouty, pressed intimately against the telephone receiver.

Maxie Corban. Crash's new sister-in-law. Alone in the guest bedroom, having telephone sex.

"Are you ready?" she whispered. "Don't hold back. Now. I want it now!"

A groan escaped Joseph. And then another.

Maxie slammed down the receiver and shot straight up in bed.

Joe froze, hoping she wouldn't see him. But her eyes were like lasers, burning holes in his.

He wished he'd gone out the other door when he'd had a chance, wished he'd been caught washing his hands, even wished he'd been caught on the toilet. Anything but this. Anything but standing in the gap of the doorway, sweat dripping off his face, his arousal evident.

"You!" she said.

She unfolded herself from the bed and stalked toward him, gloriously, magnificently naked. He didn't even try not to look.

Suddenly she realized what she was doing, and bent to retrieve her swimsuit.

If he had left then, they both might have been able to ignore the incident. They both might have pretended it had never happened.

But the lawyer in him wouldn't let him leave. He

couldn't ignore a challenge, couldn't quit the field without winning the battle. Or at least proving his innocence.

"Look," he said. "This is not what it seems."

Maxie harnessed her lush breasts in minuscule triangles of bright pink, then hopped around on one leg trying to get into her string bikini.

"Oh no? . . . Dammit." The bikini bottoms were so tangled up, she had to start all over.

"Need any help?"

It was the wrong thing to say. If he'd been in his right mind, Joe would never have made the offer, but his right mind had vanished about the time Maxie had made her first erotic suggestion on the telephone.

"Don't you dare!"

All her maneuvering made her bounce in exciting, enticing ways, ways guaranteed to prolong Joe's own painfully embarrassing condition.

"Look . . . I'm not the kind of man who does this sort of thing," he said.

"You stand there in the doorway watching me . . . watching me . . ."

"I think it's called telephone sex."

"I *know* what it's called." She finally won the battle with her clothes, and stalked toward him, hands on her hips.

"What I want to know is what were *you* doing?" Her eyes raked him from head to toe. "As if it weren't perfectly obvious."

"I was using the bathroom."

"I can see that. Using it to spy on me and get your own jollies."

Thankfully, her rage and his embarrassment combined to dampen Joe's ardor. He was almost feeling back to normal.

Almost. The thought of having to sit at the table with Crash's sister-in-law for the rest of the evening was mortifying. More than that, it was downright scary. Even now, even in the face of her fury and his acute embarrassment, he was stirred by her.

"To be perfectly blunt, I was using the toilet."

"The toilet's through there." She nodded to the doorway behind him.

"I know that." He nodded toward the sink. "I wash afterward. Don't you?"

"What is this? A lesson in etiquette? You must have flunked the course. Polite people don't spy."

"The door was cracked open."

"You didn't have to look."

"I couldn't help myself."

"Are you saying *I'm* at fault here?"

"You're very compelling on the telephone."

"I didn't know I had an audience of two."

"You're also appealing in person, I might add."

"If you're trying to flatter me into forgiveness, it won't work. I'll never forgive you for spying on me like that, Joseph Patrick Beauregard. Never!"

With that parting shot, she'd stalked off and left Joseph standing in the bathroom.

He stood in the same spot now, fully clothed, eyes closed, remembering how she'd looked that fateful summer night, magnificent in her rage, the tiny bikini setting her body off to perfection.

He'd stolen something from her, something very precious. He'd taken the gift of intimacy she bestowed on another via phone and used it for himself.

And he'd never even apologized.

Each detail of that night was emblazoned in Joe's mind. Even as he replayed it, he knew he'd missed nothing. Not once had he ever said to Maxie Corban, "I'm sorry," not once in all those months. He'd taken the coward's way out, avoiding her at every turn to cover his own embarrassment.

And now fate was forcing them back together, fate in the form of a nine-pound baby boy.

It was high time he cleared the air. He had to apologize.

Energized, Joe returned to his brother's den and dashed off a note: "Sorry I had to leave. There is something very important I have to take care of."

He propped the note on the telephone table, then riffled through the telephone book till he found Maxie's address. Should he call first?

It would be the polite thing to do. It would also give her a chance to tell him no.

Following his second impulse of the evening, Joseph headed toward Maxwell Street. Her house was yellow. And in the driveway was her little red Volkswagen as well as a navy blue Ford sedan.

She had company. Something he hadn't counted on.

Maybe he should leave. The clock on his dashboard said ten. It was too late to go calling anyhow, especially without an invitation.

Joseph had his hand on the ignition key when he saw her through the window, red hair shining in the lamplight, head thrown back, laughing. Suddenly everything he'd meant to say vanished from his mind. There was something about her so compelling that all he could do was sit and stare.

As he watched, another person came into view, a man, tall and handsome in a reckless, debonair sort of way. He snapped his fingers, did a quick cha-cha step, and Maxie joined in. They were beautiful dancing together, rhythmical, graceful.

The man was everything that would appeal to Maxie, everything Joe was not. He didn't have a debonair bone in his body and couldn't dance a step if his life depended on it.

Not that any of that mattered. He'd come to apologize to Maxie, not to woo her.

He had Susan, and she was all he needed. The sensible thing would be to drive down the street and pretend he'd never even come. After all, he would see Maxie tomorrow in his office. That would be soon enough to apologize.

He took one last glance through the window. The man swirled Maxie around the floor, then dipped low, bent over her like a lover.

Joe turned off the ignition, slammed out of the car, and barreled up the sidewalk.

As he punched the doorbell he muttered to himself, "Hell, I came to apologize. No need to turn tail and run because Fred Astaire can't keep his hands off her."

The door swung open and Maxie stood there, flushed and laughing. The strains of a sexy blues song drifted through the doorway.

"Good grief," she said, sobering. "What brings you here?"

Joe craned his neck, but he couldn't see the man she'd been dancing with. He'd probably gone to the bedroom to wait for her. Probably at this very minute he was stripping off his clothes and climbing between the covers.

At that thought every shred of good breeding deserted him.

"Do I have to tell you standing on the sidewalk, or can I come in?"

"Well, of course."

She stood back to let him pass by. She was wearing purple shorts that showed off her legs, and a patch of sweat made her tank top stick to her body in enticing ways.

His body responded instantly. Or was it his body *and* his mind? He brought himself under control and followed her into the den.

It looked like something she would design, cheerful, comfortable, and zany—sedate antique rocking chairs sharing space with chairs painted purple and sporting red painted lips and gold high-heeled shoes on the front legs; marble-topped end tables vying for attention with tables painted in pink and purple polka dots; a big, plush pink sofa topped by pillows with embroidered lips and red fringe.

That's where the man sat, on the sofa among the painted lips and red fringe.

"Joseph, this is my associate, Claude."

"Just Claude," he said, extending his hand, obviously amused by Joseph's expression.

Joseph was mad at himself for being so transparent. In the courtroom he was as inscrutable as the Lincoln Memorial. Why was it that every time he got around Maxie every ounce of civilized behavior deserted him and he reverted to a primitive jungle beast?

"So," Claude said, his smile false. "What brings you here this time of night?"

He emphasized his point by consulting his watch. Joseph rose to the challenge.

"Business," he said, his smile equally false. "Personal."

Maxie sat on the sofa close to Claude, too close, in Joe's opinion, and he chose a chair directly opposite them. He always preferred looking his opponents straight in the eye. There were two chairs opposite the sofa, but he deliberately chose the purple one with the outrageous gold high-heeled shoes. Not for one minute would he want Claude to guess that he was conservative to the bone.

Besides, he was feeling a little reckless. And more than a little proud of himself. Men who were conservative to the bone didn't pay unexpected late-night calls then sit in outrageous chairs.

Maxie looked distinctly uncomfortable. A first for

her, Joe was certain. And Claude showed no intention of leaving. He leaned toward Joe, a satisfied smirk on his face.

"Earlier this evening Maxie and I were discussing the mating habits of the praying mantis," he said.

"Claude . . ."

He reached over and patted her knee. "It's one of Maxie's favorite subjects."

Joseph saw right through the ploy. He settled back in his chair, a sizable man who had no intention of being pushed off the turf by this suave Fred Astaire clone.

"It's also one of mine," Joe said. "I'm particularly intrigued by the actions of the female." He swung his glance toward Maxie. "She devours the male."

A pink flush started at the highest point of her cheekbones and spread all the way out to her hairline. It was the only sign that she was not in control.

Her unsettled state suited Joseph's purposes just fine. Maxie in control was lethal.

A heavy silence descended over them, and for a while it looked as if all three of them would spend the rest of the evening sitting stiffly in their seats trying to stare each other down. Joe had already made up his mind that nobody was going to get the best of him this evening, certainly not Claude. He'd come to apologize, and apologize he would, even if he had to sit in the purple chair all night waiting for Claude to get the hint and leave.

"Is that before or after sex?" Claude said.

Joseph didn't bat an eyelash. He merely quirked an

eyebrow upward and plucked a peppermint out of the carnival glass bowl on the table beside him.

Maxie gathered force like a thundercloud. She practically shot sparks when she stood up.

"During, I think," she said, her smile wicked.

Joe left his peppermint suspended two inches from his open mouth, and the formerly unflappable Claude flapped into silence.

"Now, if you gentlemen will excuse me, I'm going to the kitchen to make lemonade—to cool everybody off."

She swept grandly from the room, leaving Joe and Claude staring at each other.

When the kitchen door had closed behind her, Joe stood up, a big man who didn't hesitate to use his size to his advantage when the need arose. He meandered around the room, inspecting every nook and cranny, every knickknack that would give him a clue to Maxie.

"Would you stop that prowling?" Claude said.

"Do I make you nervous, Claude?"

"No, but you're making me mad. What do you mean showing up at Maxie's like this, unannounced?"

"It's personal."

"I happen to be Maxie's best friend, and if you think I'm going to leave and let you do or say something to upset her, you're very mistaken. I might not look like much of a man, but I'm willing to take you on." Claude stood up, his fists doubled. "And anybody else who might harm her."

It was then that Joseph saw Claude for what he was. He sat back down, in the rocking chair this time.

"I've misjudged you, Claude. Only a very good friend would be willing to duke it out with a man nearly twice his size."

Claude sat back down, somewhat mollified.

"Look, Claude. I'm afraid we got off to a bad start. I came here on impulse, on an errand that is very important to me."

"Maxie and I have no secrets from each other."

"Maybe not, but what I have to say is best said without an audience."

Claude looked as if somebody had sewed him to the sofa.

"You're a stubborn son of a gun, aren't you?" he said.

"So are you."

"It looks like a stalemate."

Though Joe rarely smoked, and used his pipe mainly as a prop, it came in handy at times when he wanted to signal to his opponents that he was in the battle for the duration. He took his time tamping in tobacco and putting a match to the bowl.

"So it does," Joe said.

"Are you planning to smoke that odious thing?"

"Yes."

"This is a silk shirt I'm wearing. It will smell like tobacco."

"Probably."

"You're not going to leave, are you?"

"No." Joe took a deep puff, then settled back in his chair.

Claude picked up a magazine and fanned it around. Then with a snort of disgust he stood up.

"Tell Maxie I had to go."

"I'll do that."

At the door Claude made a parting shot. "If I didn't know Maxie could hold her own against a passel of wildcats, I'd stay on that sofa, regardless of my silk shirt. If I were you, I'd be careful what I say to her."

"I'll keep that in mind."

"See that you do."

Feeling generous at his victory, Joseph let Claude have the last word. As the door closed behind him, Joe sat back in his chair and smiled.

In the kitchen Maxie was humming.

FOUR

When Maxie was upset she hummed. Sometimes it fooled people into thinking she was not about to fall into a million pieces. Sometimes it disarmed people so that they forgot what they'd come for.

Had she put two scoops of sugar in the lemonade already? She had no earthly idea.

All she could see was the way Joseph looked sitting in her house, in her den, in her purple chair. Like something she wanted to sock with her doubled fist. Like something she wanted to eat with a spoon.

Good Lord, the man had her so confused, she didn't know if she was coming or going. She added another two scoops of sugar to the lemonade.

From the den she could hear the hum of voices. Bless Claude's dear heart. He wouldn't desert her in her time of need. He'd stick it out, no matter what Joseph Patrick Beauregard said or did.

Maxie stood on tiptoe to reach the lemonade

glasses. They were bright blue with silver stars on one side and a full moon on the other. She filled three glasses with ice cubes and poured the lemonade. Then, taking a deep breath, she arranged them on a tray and headed back into the den, back to face the music.

The murmur of voices had ceased. What did it mean? A truce? Where was Claude's acid tongue when she needed it?

She stood outside the door, gathering her courage. Then she shouldered it open.

"Ta-dah," she said.

Her dramatic entrance was greeted by an audience of one.

"You didn't have to go to all that trouble just for me."

Joseph Beauregard was a dangerous man when he smiled that way. She knew. She'd sat in the back of the courtroom once, shortly after that ill-fated summer night, watching him try a case, taking the measure of the man who had stumbled upon her most embarrassing secret.

He was lethal in the courtroom. Calm, focused, with a razor-sharp mind and rapier wit, he quietly built his case, then went in for the kill. Nothing about the consummate professional even gave hint to the man who had stood in the doorway watching her act out her fantasies.

She hesitated, studying him to see which Joseph Beauregard occupied her chair, the inscrutable litigator or the vulnerable voyeur.

"Need any help with that tray?"

The Joseph who made the offer was neither, but an entirely different man. Much to her horror, he was the Mr. Right she'd swooned over when they'd first met. He was an appealing combination of warmth and danger, of little-boy innocence and roguish charm. He was just the kind of man who set all her bells a-chiming and her hormones a-humming.

And he was strictly off-limits.

He was unapproachable not merely because he was engaged to another woman, though she certainly respected that, but because he was B. J.'s brother-in-law. That would never have stopped Maxie if she were a different kind of woman. But in spite of the fact that men and stray dogs followed her home from parties, in spite of the fact that she never had to sit home alone on Saturday night waiting for the phone to ring, she just couldn't seem to get it right with a man.

She was like that stubborn old mule her granddaddy used to plow the garden with: She wanted to gee when they wanted to haw. When they wanted marriage, she wanted fun and games. When they wanted commitment, she wanted to run. When they were thinking of a vine-covered cottage, she was thinking of a trip for two to the Bahamas.

Over the years she'd learned that there was no such thing as a friendly parting. She'd tried, goodness knew, but somebody was always storming off her porch vowing to throw himself into the Mississippi River or jump off the Empire State Building.

The longest relationship she'd ever had was long-distance. His name was Alfred Peabody, and he'd lasted six months.

As long as he was at the other end of the telephone line, things went beautifully. But the relationship had gone downhill the minute he'd come to Tupelo and tried to stake his claim.

He'd been the finest brain surgeon in California, and now he was in Africa passing out pills at a clinic.

Maxie wasn't about to be the cause of B. J.'s brother-in-law taking a slow boat to China. Face it. She was absolutely great at telephone relationships, but a dismal failure face-to-face.

Once she'd talked to B. J. about her problem, and her sister had said, "Maxie, did you ever think that maybe you're just too much woman for any man to handle? Did you ever think about moderating your ways a bit?"

She hadn't. And she wouldn't. Any man who wanted Maxie Corban would have to take her as she was. She had no intention of moderating herself for anybody.

And certainly not for Joseph Patrick Beauregard.

She sashayed across the room, putting an extra hitch in her step, and set the lemonade tray on the coffee table.

"If I'd known only you were here, I'd have added arsenic."

To her surprise, he laughed. "Smart girl. Murder should never have a witness."

"Neither should sex." It popped out before Maxie could stop herself.

Her words hung in the air while they stared at each other. She felt the heat of a blush creep up from her neck and reached for a soothing glass of lemonade. For a moment she held the cool glass to her throat, and when the heat didn't abate, she did what came naturally: She reached into the glass, plucked out an ice cube, and rubbed it across her hot chest, dipping into the neck of her tank top to skim the tops of her breasts.

"My God," he whispered.

Too late, Maxie realized she had an audience. Or had she realized it all along? Had she used the ice in a provocative manner deliberately to taunt him? To test his reaction?

Maxie dropped the half-melted cube onto the metal tray, and it was like a thunderclap to their heightened senses. She wet her bottom lip with the tip of her tongue, and Joseph squeezed the bowl of his pipe so hard, his knuckles turned white.

"Do you want some?" she said.

"Some what?"

Goose bumps rose on her arms, and she hugged herself, shivering.

"Lemonade," she said.

"No . . . yes."

Suddenly the room was the Sahara, and Joseph, a distant oasis. Her eyes never left his as she made the long, hot trek. His body heat was shocking. She stood beside his chair a full minute before either of them could move a muscle.

"Your drink."

"Thank you."

His fingertips touched hers, and she felt the shock waves through every inch of her body. Stunned, she whirled around and raced back to the safety of the sofa.

She kept several pink notepads scattered throughout the house in case she got a brilliant decorating idea or wanted to capture an elusive thought. As her hand closed around the one on the coffee table, she risked a glimpse at Joseph. He was gulping lemonade as if he hadn't had a drop of moisture in days and was in immediate danger of dehydration.

Clamping her lower lip between her teeth, she began to write.

"What are you writing?"

"Just a note to myself."

"About the party?"

"No."

She put the notebook back on the coffee table, then faced him with a smile that she hoped looked brave and perky.

"So, where's Claude?"

"He had to leave."

"It's not like him to leave without saying good-bye."

"He said to tell you good-bye."

"Did you do something to make him leave?"

"You give me too much credit."

She glanced at his empty glass. "More lemonade?"

"I'll get it."

This time he was the one who made the trek, but

he was across the room before she had time to prepare herself. He loomed over her, gorgeous and mouthwatering, and much too close for comfort. Still towering over her, he drank the lemonade intended for Claude in three big swallows.

The glass clinked as he set it back on the tray. Instead of going back to his chair on the other side of the room, he sat beside her.

His thigh brushed her bare leg, and she was certain it was a deliberate ploy to throw her off guard.

They spied the notepad at the same time, the ink in bold relief against the pale pink paper.

" 'No touching.' No touching what?"

Maxie had never been one to lie.

"You."

"Like this?" He pressed his leg closer to hers.

"Yes."

In all those years Maxie had been running when men wanted her to stay, not a single one of them had set off skyrockets under her skin with a single touch. Not one. If they had, she wouldn't have been sitting on the sofa now biting the inside of her lip to keep from reaching out and fawning over a man she couldn't have.

Joseph was off-limits. Long after he had gone and she lay in her bed all alone with her motor still running, she'd have to repeat that phrase to herself a hundred times. Maybe more.

Under no circumstances was she to forget it.

But, oh, he tempted her so.

If he stayed around much longer, there was no telling what she was liable to do. She had to scare him off. That's all there was to it, for B. J.'s sake.

"And like this," she said.

She put a hand on his chest and made slow, erotic circles. He sucked in a sharp breath, then was so still, she couldn't even hear him breathing.

She felt his body heat, even through his shirt . . . and the size and shape of his muscles, the indentation over his heart, the wonderful springiness of chest hair. Unable to resist, she let her hand glide lower, across his flat belly, and downward. Her fingernails made soft clicking sounds against his zipper.

His response was immediate. And delicious.

"If you keep that up you might learn a hard lesson." His voice was hoarse.

"What lesson?"

"Tempt a man too far and pay the consequences."

Good heavens, why wasn't he running away? Thank goodness one touch was not enough to ruin a man. If she ruined Joe, B. J. would disown her. Crash would be furious. She'd be banned from the farm and would never get to tell her godson why she'd insisted he have wallpaper with angels on zebras.

Maxie withdrew her hand, then settled not so primly into her corner of the sofa.

"That's how I'm not to touch you," she said.

He studied her the same way he did opponents in a courtroom. Sweat beaded her upper lip, trickled down the side of her face, and slid toward her cleavage. Damp tendrils clung to the back of her neck.

What was he thinking? If she knew, she could plan

her next move. Her only clue was his eyes. His gaze burned right through her.

He snaked out his arm so fast, she didn't see it coming, didn't have time to scoot away. Suddenly, she found herself crushed against him, held fast with one arm around her waist and the other tangled in her hair.

She stared at him, too stunned for words, too surprised for action. For an instant he watched her, pantherlike, mysterious, and predatory. Then he claimed her lips. He was the hunter and she was the prey. He was merciless, his lips hard and demanding, his tongue sure and insistent.

Her heart slammed against her ribs, and she thought she would turn into a Victorian lady right there in her own living room, swooning on her sofa with no hope of revival.

Somebody made murmuring sounds of pleasure. Good Lord, it was her. She was groaning with ecstasy because of the delicious ways Joseph was plundering her mouth. His hands were equally seductive. The way he caressed her was pure heaven, the erotic massage he was giving the back of her neck enough to have him declared armed and dangerous.

Her whole body was purring. And she was responding to his kiss like mad. Her tongue met his thrust for thrust. Her lips were ripe and open, devouring him.

Merciful heavens, what was she doing? Was one kiss enough to send this man off into the jungles to contemplate his toes?

And could she stop at one?

At the rate they were going, they might never stop. Which would be all right with Maxie . . . except for two little things: her sister and his fiancée.

She tried counting sheep, she tried counting backward, she tried counting the polka dots on her painted table. But nothing worked. Finally she gave herself up to him. Completely. Wantonly. Brazenly. She had neither the desire nor the willpower to stop herself. Or him.

In fact, she was so enraptured that when he pulled back she was still puckered up saying "hmmmm." It took her a while to realize that she was kissing thin air.

Enraged, she swiped at her mouth with the back of her hand and retreated to her end of the sofa.

"You forgot that one," he said.

"What?"

"That's another way you shouldn't touch me."

"Of all the arrogant, pompous jerks, you take the cake."

"I was that good, was I?"

"You weren't even close to good. On a scale of one to ten you were minus two."

Maxie jerked up her glass of lemonade and slid it down the side of her face, across her throat, and into the neck of her shirt. The cool glass did nothing to abate the heat roaring through her blood. Joseph Beauregard was more than she'd bargained for.

"Perhaps another demonstration is in order," he said.

"Don't you dare!"

She jumped off the sofa and marched to the other side of the room. Searching for something to do, she spied the stereo, still blasting away. Maxie punched the off button. Hard.

"I thought the music enhanced the mood," he said.

"I'm not in the mood for dancing."

"I wasn't speaking of dancing."

There were ways a man could look at a woman that'd drive her crazy. Joseph had it down to a science.

"I was speaking of sex," he said.

FIVE

Claude pounced the minute Maxie came to work.

"So, what did Beauregard the Bull want last night?"

"Beauregard the Bull?"

Maxie turned quickly to the chore of making coffee. She was stalling and Claude knew it, but she didn't care. She preferred not to think about what had happened the previous night.

"You know who I'm talking about. He's a clever devil. If it hadn't been for my silk shirt, I'd never have left you alone with him. Never." Claude set the cups inside the saucers. "What happened after I left?"

"Nothing much."

It was nothing much if you were the kind who called a hurricane just a little wind. Maxie still felt flushed as well as confused.

"I can take a hint." Claude huffed to the other side of the room with his coffee, leaving Maxie's on the counter. "If you didn't want to tell me, why didn't you just say so in the first place."

Maxie dumped her untouched coffee and put her arm around Claude's shoulder.

"We didn't dance, Claude."

"What else didn't you do?"

Maxie was saved by the bell. Literally. The chimes over her door tinkled, and in walked Mrs. Elmore Prescott, the most demanding woman in Tupelo. Claude was at her side instantly, turning on the charm while Maxie mentally geared herself for a long day.

"My house is a disaster. An absolute disaster. I'm so tired of yellow, I could scream." Mrs. Prescott pressed her hand over her breast, her diamonds flashing in the morning sun.

Last year, yellow had been Mrs. Prescott's favorite color. She'd wanted it in her bedroom, her bath, her sun room, and the kitchen. Maxie had tried to steer her in another direction, but she'd insisted.

Maxie led her to the sofa.

"Sit down, Mrs. Prescott. Can I get you a cup of coffee?"

"No sugar. I'm dieting." She took a sip, then made a face and added three teaspoons of sugar. "I can't stand my house another minute. You've got to do something, Maxie. Today."

Reprieve, Maxie thought. She'd be so busy at Mrs. Prescott's, she wouldn't have a single minute to think about the previous night.

❖━━━━━❖

Joseph's secretary stood in the doorway. Even after a ten-hour day she was still perfectly groomed, every hair in place, every thread on her body starched and pressed.

"Is that all for today, Joseph?"

"That's all, Jenny."

"What about this six o'clock appointment?" Jenny consulted her notes. "Maxie Corban?"

Joseph felt the heat rise under his collar. Could Jenny read his face? She'd been his secretary for sixteen years. Sometimes he thought she knew him better than his mother did. He resisted the urge to leap from his chair and stand with his back to her.

"I won't need notes on that meeting. It's personal."

Jenny would never comment on his personal life unless he asked, but she couldn't contain her look of surprise.

"She's Joe's other godparent," he explained. "We're planning the baby's party."

"A bachelor party?" Jenny quipped.

"Sort of. If baby Joe's anything like my brother, he'll be throwing his own by the time he's two."

Jenny closed her steno pad. "Have a good evening, Joseph."

"You, too, Jenny."

The hands on the clock said five forty-five. Fifteen minutes till Maxie showed up, fifteen minutes to wish he had suggested breakfast or lunch or even dinner. Something in a public place. Anything, anywhere except in the privacy of his office.

He must have been insane to ask her to come there after hours. Maybe if he stayed behind his desk, nothing would happen. Maybe if he kept one hand on a pen and the other on a notepad, he could stay out of trouble.

He glanced at his watch. Ten more minutes. An eternity to think about what had happened the night before and why. And exactly what he was going to do about it.

When Maxie faced a difficult task, she dressed fit to kill. For her visit to Joseph's office she'd put on a black spandex miniskirt and red silk blouse, then picked her sexiest, most revealing undergarments, the ones she'd just purchased. Not that she planned on anybody seeing them. Feminine underwear made her feel powerful and self-confident. B. J. had once told Maxie that she spent enough money at Victoria's Secret to add a wing to her small house on Maxwell Street.

Maxie had staunchly defended her purchases. "Red lace is my secret weapon," she'd said.

Driving toward Joseph's office, she regretted her secret weapon. When she was stressed, lace made her itch. Left too long against her skin, it caused hives.

She turned the air conditioner on high, hoping the blast of arctic air would cool her itch, but a block later, she knew it was hopeless. Sighing, she pulled into a service station on the corner.

Minutes later she was at Joseph's office, itchless and devoid of motives, as well as a few essentials.

His nameplate was on the door, engraved in gold. Joseph Patrick Beauregard, Attorney at Law.

Maxie pressed her hand over her stomach. Butterflies. She hadn't had them since she'd played the role of Daisy Mae in her high school production of *Li'l Abner*.

What role was she playing now? she wondered.

Maxie Corban, godmother? Maxie Corban, sister? Maxie Corban, sister-in-law? Maxie Corban, party planner extraordinaire? Maxie Corban, vamp?

That was certainly the role she'd played in her house the previous night. Shameless hussy. Wicked seductress.

It had all started as a game. She'd never meant to do anything except scare Joseph off, and maybe pay him back for standing in the doorway watching her have telephone sex.

That's how it had started when she'd run her hands over his chest. Her motives had begun to get hazy when she'd trailed her fingertips across his groin. And when he'd kissed her, all reason had vanished.

And after that . . . She leaned against the door, remembering. . . .

"This is not about dancing," he said. "It's about sex."

They watched each other, breathless, suspended. She didn't know who made the first move, but suddenly she was in his arms, in his lap, her arms and legs wrapped around him, lips melded on his, making soft kittenish sounds of pleasure as his hands roamed all over her.

Nothing in her past had prepared her for the passion she felt, the need to consume and be consumed. She'd kissed her share of men, certainly. But she'd always been in charge. She'd always been the one to draw the line.

In Joseph's arms she didn't know a line from a circle. What was more, she didn't care. All she knew was that he held her spellbound. She forgot every vow she'd made to herself about not being the ruination of Joseph Patrick Beauregard.

He pulled her tank top out from the waistband of her shorts and slid his hands underneath, and she didn't make a sound of protest, not even a whimper.

"That feels glorious. Ohhh, I want more."

His eyes were dark and mysterious, glowing as if candles were lit deep inside them.

"More?" he whispered.

"Yes. I want . . ." Her body hummed. She hardly knew what she wanted, only that Joseph was the one who could provide it.

He raked her tank top off her shoulders and crumpled it around her waist. His breath was hot on her nipples, his tongue delicious, his mouth heavenly. Clinging to him, she arched her back, giving him easy access. She was liquid fire, burning, melting.

"Oh yes," she said.

"You like that, don't you?"

"I love that . . . I want more."

He lowered her to the sofa. The cushions were soft, Joseph, hard. And oh so right. So very right.

His hands slid between her legs, underneath the leg of her shorts.

"You're so wet."

"Because of you. Only you."

His mouth claimed hers and, petallike, she parted for the delicious exploration of his fingers. There was magic in his touch, the kind of magic that set off skyrockets and caused stars to fall. All reason vanished. Maxie encouraged him with eyes and lips and hands, with soft murmurings and whisper-light caresses and kisses as gentle as a melting snowflake.

Suddenly she arched toward his questing hand, crying out, her body melting, exploding. Still spinning, she fell back, her arms wrapped tightly around him, his lips pressed against her temple.

She reached for his zipper, he reached for hers. Panting, writhing, they freed each other.

"Yes, yes, yes," she said, guiding him home.

The stars fell one by one as the tip of his shaft dipped lightly inside her. Her whole body zinged, and she was sky-borne, spiraling upward.

"I want you, Joseph," she whispered. "All of you."

His whole body went rigid. "My God," he whispered. "Susan."

He pulled back, leaving her bereft and hungry. And furious.

"The name is Maxie."

She shoved him off and reached for her clothes.

"Here, let me." He tried to help, but she slapped

his hands away and retreated to the opposite side of the room.

"Leave," she said.

"Not yet. Not till I do what I came for."

"I think you've already done enough."

"I came to apologize."

"You call *that* an apology?"

"I didn't mean for that to happen."

Neither had she, but she wasn't about to tell him so. That would be admitting that she'd been totally out of control.

"Well, it did," she said. "Fortunately, I stopped it before it had gone too far."

He didn't contradict her. If he had, she'd have bashed the lemonade tray over his head.

"I have a fiancée. Her name is Susan."

He'd unbuttoned his shirt—or had she?—and he sat on the sofa with a great deal of naked chest showing, all of it gorgeous. She wasn't about to give him the satisfaction of looking away. Let him think the sight of all that muscle and crisp dark hair didn't tempt her.

"I don't care if her name is Mergatroid. Just leave."

"Not until I do what I came for."

"Good grief. You are the most stubborn man I've ever known."

"Probably."

At last he fastened his shirt. She noted with some satisfaction that his hands shook. Not much, but enough to tell her that Joseph Patrick Beauregard wasn't completely unmoved by that near-heavenly experience on her sofa.

Suddenly she realized she was hovering on the far side of the room in a cowardly fashion. As if *she* were the one to blame. Bent on revenge she stalked across the room.

Nothing is more dangerous than a woman spurned. She plopped down beside him. Close. So close her left leg smashed up against his right thigh.

A bead of sweat popped out along his upper lip. She took note with wicked glee.

"So, Joseph . . ." She ran her hands lightly along his thigh, and was rewarded with another bead of sweat, this one sliding down his cheek. "What kind of apology do you have in mind this time?" She leaned in close, deliberately brushing her breast against his upper arm. "Something kinky?"

He didn't shift away. She would have to give him that. As a matter of fact, he reached for her hand. Since she'd been the one to so brazenly demand all this touching, there was no way she could pull out of his grasp.

"Nothing kinky. Though the idea does have merit."

His smile was somewhat lopsided and totally disarming. Good grief, how many facets did this man have? And why did she find every one of them charming?

He held her hand lightly, as if it were a baby bird nesting in his palm.

"Maxie, I came here tonight to apologize for what

happened nine months ago. I never meant to stand in the doorway watching you. It just happened. And I'm sorry. I invaded your privacy, and for that I apologize."

She felt foolishly close to tears. "Apology accepted," she said, clearing her throat.

"As for tonight . . ."

His thumb circled her palm, sending tingles along her spine. If he apologized for what happened on her sofa, she would cry. That's all there was to it. She would burst into tears in her own living room, and once she got on a crying jag she was like her sister: She had a hard time stopping. It would be messier than floodwaters from the Nile.

"I can neither explain nor apologize. All I can do is assure you that it wasn't planned . . . and it won't happen again."

It won't happen again.

With his parting words echoing in her mind, Maxie traced the cool lettering on his nameplate.

"You're right, Joseph Beauregard. It won't happen again."

Taking a deep breath, she pushed open the door and stepped inside his office.

SIX

Nothing had prepared him for the sight of Maxie. Not the stern lecture he'd given himself, not his feeble attempts to rationalize what had happened on her sofa, and certainly not his staunch resolutions never to be moved by her again. The sight of her stirred him beyond his wildest imaginings. Her lips alone were enough to make his lower body stand up and salute.

Lush and vivid, they made a perfect, inviting circle when she spoke.

"Hello, Joe."

He reached for something to hang on to, anything. The brass letter opener was cool in his hand. But not cool enough.

Maxie was leaning against his credenza, hip slung, short skirt showing off a delicious length of extremely gorgeous legs, red silk blouse clinging like a second skin.

He wanted to slam the door shut, turn the key, and

romp all over his office with her. On top of the desk, under the desk, in the swivel chair, on the carpet, against the credenza.

He had gone stark raving mad. That was it. He'd entered some sort of pre-midlife crisis when all his values were turned upside down, when everything he'd always believed in no longer had meaning.

"Aren't you going to ask me to sit down?"

He felt a rush of relief. Standing she was dynamite. Sitting she'd be partially hidden behind his desk. He would concentrate on her face.

That was it. He'd look at her face . . . except for the lips. Best to avoid the lethal lips.

"Please. Sit down."

Manners dictated that he show her to a chair. A leather wing back. A man's chair. Tall and sturdy.

When Maxie sat down, her skirt hiked dangerously high. So did his blood pressure.

His legs felt like wet noodles, and he sank into the chair facing her. Her fragrance washed over him, an exotic brew that intoxicated him. It made him think of sex beside a waterfall in the jungles of South America. And he'd never even been to South America. He wondered why not. Certainly he was wealthy enough to go anyplace he wanted, do anything he desired.

There were a lot of things he'd never done. For instance, sex beside a waterfall.

"Sex."

"Did you say something?" Maxie said.

He cleared his throat. "Six. We have only six weeks till the party."

"I know. I thought I'd save us some time by putting a few ideas on paper."

"That's a good idea."

"If you'll just check the ones you like, I'll have Claude pick it up tomorrow. Or you can mail it to me."

Disappointment slashed him. She was giving him the brush-off. Who could blame her? Especially after last night.

"Now where did I put that list?"

She pawed through her purse. One by one she plopped its contents onto the top of his desk: a flacon of perfume, lipstick, hand mirror, car keys, ticket stubs to *Michael*, sales slips, a small pair of scissors, one black stocking. Maxie Corban had to be the most disorganized person he'd ever known.

And he found her totally fascinating.

Suddenly she snagged an item deep in her purse and sailed it toward his desktop. A wisp of red lace. The tiniest pair of bikini panties he'd ever seen.

"It's not in here," she said, glancing up at him, her smile totally innocent and completely enchanting. "I've lost it."

He dragged his attention away from the telltale red lace. "Maybe you've only misplaced it. Weren't you carrying a briefcase when you came in?"

"Of course . . . that's it."

There was no way to describe the way she crossed the room. Every provocative inch of her swayed in a most inviting way. He got dizzy just looking at her.

Her briefcase was on the floor. Maxie didn't squat

and pick it up, she bent at the waist and leaned over. Riveted, Joseph watched. The skirt tightened across her hips and her behind . . . and there was no visible panty line.

"Here it is," she said, bending lower to snatch her list from the briefcase.

In that fraction of a second, Joe almost lost control. Maxie gave new meaning to the term "free spirit." She'd gone to the limits of propriety—and beyond.

"I have it." She sashayed across the room, smiling.

"You surely do." He sounded like a bullfrog in heat, but it was the only voice he had at the moment, and was darned lucky to have even that.

"Do you want to see it?"

"I already have . . ." He gripped the arms of the chair, his mind awhirl. He cleared his throat. "I already have a few ideas of my own."

Maxie placed her list in his lap. He hoped she didn't notice his condition. Then she sat down facing him and crossed her legs, her skirt dangerously high.

"You look uncomfortable," she said. "Is it something I said?"

"It's hot in here."

Her smile was wicked. It was then that Joe knew she'd been toying with him. She'd deliberately set him up.

And why not? After the night before, what woman in her right mind wouldn't be out for a little revenge. He'd waved a red flag, and Maxie had charged out of the gate looking for first blood.

Joseph loved nothing better than a challenge. What better way to respond to Maxie than to give her a dose of her own medicine. He loosened his tie and tossed it onto his desk, right on top of her red panties.

"Ahh, that's better." He smiled at her. "Feel free to take off anything you like."

"I'm fine, thank you." She uncrossed her legs, and tugged at the edge of her skirt.

"Are you sure?"

"Certainly."

"Of course you are." He took his time getting out of the chair, partially for effect but mostly because of his condition. He snagged her panties off his desk. "You've already relieved yourself of a few items."

She reached for the wisp of lace, but he held them out of her grasp.

"Were you hot when you took these off?" He twirled the panties aloft. "What made you so hot, Maxie? Who were you thinking of when you discarded your underwear?"

Joseph had been in enough courtrooms to master the art of reading the opponent. Not only was Maxie a good actress, but she was unpredictable. That was one of the reasons he found her so exciting. In the staid, conventional world of law, Maxie was a breath of fresh air. No, more than a breath. She was a hurricane.

"Certainly not you." She jumped out of her chair and stalked toward the door.

"Maxie." Joe held her panties aloft. "You forgot these."

"Did you think I was leaving?" She jerked her

briefcase off the floor, then huffed back to her chair and sat down. "Don't you have anything better to do than fondle my panties?"

"What did you have in mind?"

"Not what you're thinking."

"And what is that?"

She appraised him leisurely, lingering longest at his groin. A slow, wicked grin split her face.

"You're a big boy." She wet her lips with the tip of her tongue. "You figure it out."

Adrenaline shot through Joe. He had finally met his match, a woman who could parry every verbal thrust. Gleeful, he moved in on her. She didn't budge an inch, even when he stood so close, his thigh brushed hers.

"Could it be we're thinking the same thing, Maxie?"

He dropped to his knees in front of her, pinning her to the chair. With one hand across her bare thighs, he reached for the front of her red blouse. His fingers delved inside and lightly caressed her rigid nipples.

"Do you always go braless? Or only when you visit me?"

"What would you do if I said this is all for you, Joe?" She leaned closer, her breath hot against his cheek. "Would you do the same thing you did last night?"

The game they were playing had become dangerous. Her question was a double-edged sword. Did she mean "Would you make love to me?" or "Would you start something and not finish?" *No* could be an insult or a promise. *Yes* could mean he was foolhardy or cowardly.

There was only one thing to do, only one way he could possibly answer her.

"Would you?"

He could see the indecision in her eyes. If it wasn't a victory, it was at least a stalemate.

He stood his ground, knowing that the last one to break contact would be the winner. That was his rationale for continuing to kneel at her feet, touching her as intimately as a lover.

"All right," she finally said. "You've made your point. You can go back and sit down now."

"It's not that easy, Maxie."

"What do you want now? A pound of flesh?"

"No. A truce."

"That's all?"

"You don't believe me?"

"They say you can't trust a lawyer."

"Your own sister is a lawyer."

"That's different."

Suddenly Joseph stood up, laughing. "Maxie, you are the most indomitable, illogical person I've ever met."

"You forgot inappropriate."

"Inappropriate?"

"That's what you said about me that night at Crash and B. J.'s first wedding dinner."

"I told you that?"

"No. You told your brother." She placed her briefcase primly in her lap. "I eavesdrop too."

"Maxie, you're appropriate for carousels and circuses and trips to never-never land."

"But not for lawyers," she added, her voice matter-of-fact. "Now, shall we get on with the party plans? After all, that's what I came for."

"Did you, Maxie?"

She became a whirlwind, all flying red hair, blazing eyes, and flashing legs. With one swipe at the desktop, she raked her belongings back into her purse, then slung her bag over her shoulder, jerked up her briefcase, and marched to the door.

"What about the party?" he said.

"It will be in Crash and B. J.'s living room. I'll decorate my half and you decorate yours. I'll serve my food and you serve yours. I'll make my speech and you make yours."

Her body rigid with rage, she saluted. Then she slammed the door so hard, it rocked on its hinges.

Joseph went to the window and watched her get into her car. It was a sight worthy of awed silence. He stood there long after her car had disappeared, watching the play of the streetlights on the dark streets.

"That's one hell of a woman," he said.

SEVEN

The scent of flowers was overpowering. They were everywhere, on the windowsill, on the countertop, flanking the door, on the bedside table.

Lying in the narrow hospital bed surrounded by bouquets from her adoring husband, B. J. looked like a queen.

Maxie wished she hadn't come. She felt like a party pooper. Dragging a chair to the bedside, she forced cheer into her voice.

"So, how's the new mother?"

"I'm great, but you look like a cat that's lost eight of its lives. What's wrong?"

Maxie sighed. She could never fool her sister.

"Nothing."

"Who are you kidding? Even that sensational outfit can't disguise the fact that you're in the doldrums. Where've you been, dressed like that, anyhow? Auditioning for something?"

"I guess you could call it that."

Maxie plucked a rose out of the vase on the bedside table and put it between her teeth. Then she twirled around the room.

"Just call me Gypsy Rose Lee."

"The stripper? Don't tell me. You ditched your underwear again."

"Had to. It was driving me crazy."

"And then?"

"Then what?"

"Come on, Maxie. There's more to the story. What's the real reason you came up here tonight looking as if somebody's put out a contract and you're the target?"

"That's what I feel like. The target."

"Whose?"

"You're not going to like this."

"Try me."

"Joseph's."

"Joe? Not Joe. Come on, you've got to be kidding."

"Maybe exaggerating a little."

"That's no news flash. You always exaggerate. Drama is in your blood." B. J. patted the covers on her bed. "Hop up here and we'll have one of those sister-to-sister talks we both can't live without."

Maxie tucked the rose back into the vase and hopped onto the bed. B. J. giggled like a teenager. It was wonderful to see her sister so happy. Up until fate had plopped Joseph smack into the middle of her life, Maxie had been happy.

Or at least she'd thought so. Now she didn't know happy from sad, right from left, up from down.

"Okay, tell your story—with as little exaggeration as possible, please."

"I had a meeting with Joe tonight to plan the baby's party. . . . No, wait. . . . That's not the beginning. It all started last night. . . . No. That's not right, either."

"This sounds serious." B. J. studied her sister closely. "Maxie, what's going on between you and my brother-in-law?"

"Nothing. I swear to you, nothing is going on between us."

"Whoa. You don't have to sound so defensive."

"I'm not defensive."

"Yes, you are. You act as if I'm going to bite your head off or something."

"Or something. Kill me, maybe. Or string me up by the toes to a magnolia tree and leave me for the birds to peck out my eyes and all my good parts."

"Good grief. I never heard of anything so ridiculous. Why would I want to do something like that to my own sister?"

"Because I'm going to ruin your beloved brother-in-law."

"You're going to ruin Joe? Good Lord, Maxie. What's the matter with you? He's one of the nicest, kindest, most decent men I've ever known. There's not a mean bone in his body. He's smart too. And successful."

B. J. was so upset, she overturned the water pitcher

on her bedside table. Maxie got a towel out of the bathroom and swabbed up the mess.

"See. That's what I'm talking about. Just the mention of his name linked with mine and you're ready to send me to Outer Mongolia."

"Now, wait a minute. You didn't say anything about the two of you together. You said you were going to ruin him."

"I ruin every man who comes near me."

B. J. was not a first-rate attorney for nothing. Maxie's scattered approach to a subject sometimes clouded the issue, but it didn't take B. J. long to sort through the extraneous details and get to the heart of the matter.

"Are you telling me that you've fallen for Joe?"

"I didn't say that." Plopping back onto the bed, Maxie threw up a smoke screen. "How can you possibly think that?"

"Years in a courtroom taught me to read face and body language. Besides, you never could hide your feelings, Maxie."

"Well, you've read wrong. Joseph Beauregard is not at all the kind of man I go for." She hoped B. J. didn't see her fingers crossed behind her back.

B. J. studied her sister. "Joe could use a little less control and a little more spontaneity in his life."

"I thought you thought he was perfect."

"He is." B. J. reached for her sister's hand. "But so are you."

"He's not the sort of man I want to ting-a-ling with."

"What?"

Maxie laughed. "Just an expression of Claude's."

"You know, Maxie, I don't like to talk about your choices in men, but I do wish you'd pick somebody nice like Joe."

"He's engaged. Besides, we're complete opposites. He's conservative mid-America in a button-down collar, a three-piece suit, and a striped tie. I'm Tahiti in a grass skirt and a coconut-shell bra with a headdress of peacock feathers. He's earth, I'm air. He's water, I'm fire. He's . . ."

"I didn't say *Joe*, I said somebody like him. You always fall for scalawags."

"They're decent men until I finish with them. Then they end up on sabbatical in the frozen tundra."

"What about that CPA you dated? Isn't he still in Tupelo? He seemed like the reliable sort."

"He has a terrible flaw."

"What?"

"He wears saddle oxfords and thinks Julia Roberts was a gourmet cook on a television show."

"I'm horrified." B. J. pretended horror, and Maxie grinned.

"When's the wedding?"

"Whose wedding?"

"Joseph's."

"Heaven only knows. They've postponed it six times, three each. They've been engaged for five years."

"Good heavens." Maxie pretended a big yawn to hide her glee.

"It's not exactly a sizzling love match. Poor Joe."

"What's she like?"

"Who?"

"Joseph's fiancée."

"What's with all these questions? I thought the two of you didn't gee haw."

"We don't. Just idle curiosity. That's all."

"Be careful, Maxie. Curiosity killed the cat."

EIGHT

Joseph was too busy to see Susan for the next two days, which was a very good thing. That gave him time to decide exactly what he was going to do when he saw her, exactly what he was going to say.

Under the guise of working on a brief, he spent long hours at his office, sitting at his desk with reams of files spread before him. But it wasn't the files he stared at, it was a wisp of red lace he'd found in his pocket the day Maxie left, a bit of froth that sent his blood pressure sky-high every time he looked at it or touched it.

Two things were clear to Joseph: His engagement was a farce, and he'd taken leave of his senses.

He'd never been indecisive, but since fate had thrust Maxie into his life he couldn't decide even the simplest things, such as whether to have wheat cereal or oatmeal for breakfast, whether to wear the navy pinstriped tie or the green one, whether to watch the news on NBC or CBS.

His take-out pizza arrived, and he was distracted from the wisp of red lace while he paid the delivery boy and ate his late dinner.

He'd just bitten in to the first slice when somebody knocked on his door. Probably the pizza boy, forgetting something.

"The door's open," he said, and in walked the last person on earth he wanted to see. If Joseph had any doubts about Susan, his feelings dispelled them. He had to do something about his engagement.

"I know you weren't expecting me," she said, "but we have to talk."

"You're right, Susan. We have to talk." He escorted her to a chair, then sat behind his desk, a sure signal that he had already begun the process of separation.

She didn't seem to mind that he hadn't greeted her with a kiss or a hug. In fact, she didn't even seem to notice.

A sadness swept over him as he realized that he couldn't remember a moment in their relationship when touching Susan had been an irresistible impulse rather than a conscious decision.

"I've come about our wedding, Joseph."

It was the perfect opening. He wondered if, after all, there was such a thing as fate.

"Yes. We need to discuss that."

"I can't possibly plan a wedding by December. My patient load has almost doubled in the last six months.

Would you mind terribly if we postponed it awhile? Say, until sometime next year?"

"Susan, how many times have we postponed this wedding?"

"I've lost count."

"Well, I haven't. We've postponed it six times. This will be the seventh. Does that tell you something?"

"What are you driving at, Joseph?"

"Did you ever think that perhaps we're not right for each other?"

"We're perfect together, Joseph. Exactly alike."

"Maybe that's our problem. We're too much alike. Maybe we need balance."

"Are you feeling well, Joseph? You've never talked like this before."

That was because he'd never felt like this before. Analytical to the bone, he could decipher a legal problem with ease, calculate all the angles with alacrity, put together a brilliant brief while most attorneys were still doing their homework. But when it came to matters of the heart, Joseph was lost. He had believed that finding the right woman was as simple as analyzing all her qualities to see if they were compatible with his needs.

What he hadn't counted on was a woman who could fire his blood with a single look, a woman who could stir his passion by a movement as simple as crossing her legs, a woman who could drive him crazy merely by being in the same room. What he hadn't bargained for was Maxie.

He wanted to do the fair thing. He didn't want to hurt Susan. He didn't want to back out on promises.

But most of all he didn't want to spend the rest of his life wondering if he'd made the right choice.

"Susan, did you ever think that you might want something different? Somebody not so predictable?"

"No." She twisted the ring on her finger. The two-carat emerald-cut diamond caught the light and shot sparks across his desktop. "I don't like to be surprised. I like to be in control of every aspect of my life. I always know where you are, what you're doing, what's going to happen next. You're dependable, Joseph."

"But do you love me, Susan? Not in an intellectual way, but in a way that makes you lose your breath when I walk into a room."

Susan was an exceptionally intelligent woman and a brilliant psychiatrist. She squared her shoulders and looked at him, not as a lover but as a doctor to a patient. She didn't speak for a long time, but sat quietly in her chair observing him.

"You've met someone, haven't you, Joseph?"

"Yes and no. She's someone I knew several months ago, but circumstances have brought her back into my life, and suddenly I'm questioning everything I'd ever believed about love and marriage."

"I'm going to ask you one question, and I want you to be perfectly frank with me. Do you think this is a temporary condition?"

Susan was really asking him if the two of them had a future. She was saying that she was willing to wait long enough for him to get this nonsense out of his system.

Joseph honestly didn't know. All he knew was that it would be terribly unfair to keep Susan dangling while he found out whether Maxie was a passing fancy, whether she was like some exotic fruit he had to taste before he could be content with pot roast and mashed potatoes.

He had no intention of keeping Susan in an emotional limbo.

"No," he said. "I don't believe it's a temporary condition."

"I see." Susan twisted the diamond around her finger, then slipped it off and set it on the edge of the desk. "Thanks for being honest with me, Joseph. You're a good man." She stood up and kissed his cheek. "I wish you well."

"You, too, Susan."

He hadn't expected hysterics from her, nor even tears. But her total lack of emotion told him more than anything about their relationship: It was a meeting of minds, not a joining of hearts.

At the door she turned. "If things don't work out the way you expect, call me, Joseph." Her smile was bittersweet. "Not to take up where we left off, but just to talk. . . . I'll waive my usual fee."

"Thanks, Susan. You're a class act."

After she had gone Joseph sat at his desk a long time, thinking.

How to woo a wildcat, that was the question. Domesticate her? Tame her?

One thing was certain: He had no intention of doing to her what he had done to Susan. Before he made any decisions about his future, he had to find out exactly who he was.

Obviously he was not the archconservative he'd always believed. Maxie had awakened something wild in him, and he had to find out just how deep that wildness went and just how far it would take him.

"Did Joseph call today?"

Maxie dropped Mrs. Elmore Prescott's portfolio onto the drafting table, then plopped onto the sofa, kicked off her shoes, and propped her feet up.

"That's the first thing you've asked every day for the last three days, and no, he didn't call."

"Did his secretary call?"

"His secretary didn't call, his accountant didn't call, his legal assistant didn't call, even his mother didn't call. Nobody from the office of Joseph Patrick Beauregard called."

"I deserved that."

Claude sat beside her and kicked off his loafers. "No, you didn't, dear. I'm just being a bitch."

Maxie raked her fingers through her hair. "It's been a long week. Mrs. Prescott's bathroom is driving me crazy, B. J. is watching over me like a mother hen, and I don't have a clue whether baby Joe's party will ever come together."

"Let's do something wild tonight," he said. "Something that will make us forget this crazy week."

"There's a country-western band at Bogart's."

"Can I wear my red western boots?"

"Will they clash with my purple ones?"

The two old friends threw back their heads and laughed.

"Maxie, are you sure Bogart's is ready for us?"

"It doesn't matter, Claude. We're ready for them."

What Maxie wasn't ready for was the man who walked through the door of Bogart's right in the middle of "Jukebox Saturday Night."

"You stepped on my boots, Maxie."

"Sorry, Claude."

"Is something wrong?"

"Look who just walked through the door."

"My Lord. He's wearing jeans. I thought he never went anywhere without his three-piece suit."

It wasn't Joseph's clothes that had Maxie's attention, it was the woman on his arm. Tall, blond, and flashy, she was definitely not his fiancée, not unless Susan had grown two inches taller, bleached her hair, and had breast implants.

"Who is that woman?" she said.

"I don't know, but she's not my type. I would never have guessed she was his." Claude spun her around the polished dance floor. "Is she yours?"

Maxie roared with laughter. "You're not only the best dancer in Tupelo, you're also the wittiest. Did you know that, Claude?"

"Certainly."

The song ended, and the band segued into a slow ballad.

"Do you want to go somewhere else, Maxie?"

"Are you kidding? I'm not about to let that man spoil my fun."

Maxie watched as Joseph and his date found a table in a dark corner. She imagined all sorts of deliciously wicked things Joseph could do under the table-cloth . . . but not to her. After all, he considered her inappropriate.

"I'll show him inappropriate," she said.

"Maxie, where are you going?" Claude hurried after her. "Maxie? . . . Good grief, what are you going to do?"

"Just stand back and watch. And Claude, if I land in jail, post my bail. Okay?"

NINE

"Mr. B!" Hazel dropped her dust cloth and held her hand over her heart. "Lordy, you scared me to death." The hall clock bonged four. "Are you sick or something?"

"Or something, Hazel." Joseph hung his jacket in the hall closet and loosened his tie. "I decided to come home early today."

"It's about time." She picked up her cloth and resumed her dusting. "Most folks think you live down there at that office. Some of them even ask me about it."

"Some people have nothing better to do than indulge in idle gossip." Joseph kissed her cheek. "Not you, of course, Hazel."

"They see your car parked down there on Broadway, that's all. You know me, Mr. B. They don't get a thing out of me. Not even the time of day."

Hazel picked up the mail and handed it to him, a

large red envelope. "This came today. Special delivery."

Who would send him a letter in a red envelope? One person popped immediately into his mind. He turned the envelope over, and sure enough, there it was, Magic Maxie's logo.

Smiling, he crammed the envelope into his pocket.

"I made some lemon icebox pie today. Do you want me to fix you some?"

"It sounds wonderful, but I'll get it." The envelope was burning a hole in his pocket. "Take the rest of the day off, Hazel."

"I haven't dusted the library."

"It can wait. Everybody deserves a break now and then."

"Thanks, Mr. B. I don't care if folks do call you a tightass. In my book, you're as good as they come."

"Folks call me a tightass, do they?"

"Lordy, I ought to cut my tongue out. I shouldn't have said that."

"Hazel, when have you ever been less than blunt?" He took the dust cloth, then got her jacket from the hall closet. "That's one of the reasons I need you—to keep me in line."

"I can tell you one thing, the way you were squiring that flashy woman around at Bogart's last night, it won't be long before folks will be calling you a Don Juan. It's about time too." Hazel slid into her jacket, then squashed her black straw hat on top of her head.

"How did you acquire that bit of information, may I ask?"

"My sister. Her daughter Ruthie waits tables down there. 'Night, Mr. B. See you tomorrow."

As Hazel's ancient green Cadillac pulled out of the driveway, Joseph cut himself a generous slice of pie, then settled down at the kitchen table.

He put the red envelope on the table in plain sight, then dug into his pie. Eating dessert before dinner. It was a small defiance, another way of breaking his own rules. And it felt good. Damned good.

The red envelope lay on his table, a vivid reminder of the woman who had sent it. He wondered what she'd think if she knew people were calling him a Don Juan.

It didn't matter what she thought. His visit to Bogart's had taught him something: Maxie was out of his league. Theirs wasn't merely a difference in lifestyle: They didn't even inhabit the same planet.

He tore into the envelope and spread her letter on the table.

"Joseph," it read. "I won't address you as dear because there's nothing endearing about you."

He chuckled. Maxie had revealed herself with one single line. She was still furious at him. And with good cause.

He wondered if he would ever be able to persuade her to think of him as anything except the enemy.

Still chuckling, he continued reading her letter.

"Since you haven't bothered to return my checklist of party suggestions, I assume that you absolutely hate everything I'm planning for Baby Joe. Good! I'm equally certain that I'm going to hate everything you plan."

When Maxie got hot, she was *very* hot. The letter practically scorched Joseph's hand. He poured himself a cool glass of lemonade and drank the whole thing before he returned to her letter.

"I'm going over to B. J.'s Saturday morning to get some ideas for the decorations. I'm going to use lively colors, red and yellow and purple. I'm sure you're going to want something conservative. Sorry. When I was at the store I asked about gray pinstriped balloons. They don't make them.

"The only thing pinstriped I can think of is a zebra. Do you know where we can get an angel to ride it? I would volunteer for the job, but as you know, I'm no angel. Maxie."

Joseph hooted with laughter. "You can say that again, Maxie."

Maxie Corban was many things, but angelic was not one of them. Joseph carried the letter to his library and unlocked the bottom left-hand drawer of his mahogany desk. There were only two items in the drawer, and he placed them both on top of his desk, a wisp of red lace and a gold sequined high-heeled shoe, both compliments of Maxie.

He was immersed in memories when the doorbell rang. It was Crash.

"Great jumping jelly beans, what are you doing carrying a woman's shoe?"

Until Crash pointed out the obvious, Joe wasn't even aware he clutched Maxie's shoe.

"It's a long story."

"I've got a little time. B. J. and the baby are home napping."

"How are they doing?"

"Great. Have you got anything to eat? I'm starving."

"Hazel made lemon icebox pie."

"Lead me to it."

Joseph set the shoe on the table and cut a slice of pie while Crash rummaged for a plate and fork.

"Might as well put two slices for starters." Crash picked up his fork. "Whose shoe is it? Anybody I know?"

"You know her."

"Susan wouldn't be caught dead in that shoe." Crash held it up to the light, and it sparkled. "Don't keep me in suspense. Whose is it?"

"Maxie's."

"Maxie!" Crash quirked an eyebrow. "She left her shoes at your house? I thought the two of you didn't gee haw."

"We don't. She threw it at me last night at Bogart's."

Joseph grinned at his brother's expression. He'd always been the staid, steady one, the one who never surprised a soul. It tickled him that for once he'd left Crash speechless.

"You're kidding me. Right?"

Joseph pulled out his chair, then plucked the shoe out of his brother's hand.

"Actually, she wasn't aiming at me, but I caught it anyhow."

Crash completely forgot about his pie. Propping his elbows on the table, he leaned toward his brother.

"Are you going to make me drag this story out of you bit by bit?"

"It all started last night when I took Letty Grimseley to Bogart's. . . ."

Still holding Maxie's shoe, Joe leaned back in his chair and told his brother the story, the edited version.

"Maxie was there, with Claude, both of them dancing up a storm. That woman has more moves than a cat on a hot tin roof."

Joseph got hot just thinking about the way she'd moved on the dance floor. And what he was feeling the day after was nothing compared to what he'd felt sitting at a corner table watching Maxie in the living, pulsating flesh.

"After she finished her dance, I thought she and Claude were going to leave. She'd spotted me. As you probably know, I top her list of people she'd like to push over a cliff."

"That's our Maxie." Grinning, Crash dug into his pie with gusto. "Keep talking. Don't mind if I snack. This is delicious."

"Suddenly she turned around and marched toward the bandstand. Before I knew it, she was center stage, belting out a song."

"I didn't even know she could sing."

"I don't think there's anything that woman can't do."

Not only was Maxie singing, but she was singing well, in a throaty, sexy voice that had every man in Bogart's spellbound. Joseph was jealous of them all.

"What was she singing?"

" 'Hard Hearted Hannah.' "

". . . the vamp of Savannah." Crash slapped his thigh, laughing. "Great balls of fire, that must have been something."

"It was. And it got better when she started to strip."

"She stripped? In Tupelo, Mississippi?"

"Not all the way, but enough."

"Enough for what?"

Enough to make Joseph completely forget that he'd brought another woman to Bogart's. Enough to give him ideas he'd never had before. Enough to make sitting at his table an act of sheer will.

She'd started with her jacket, a spangled and fringed bolero. Purple. Folks might have thought she was merely too hot if it hadn't been for the way she got out of the thing. Slowly. Sensuously. Maxie's movements had put Joe in mind of a tigress on the prowl. She had actually purred into the mike while she'd removed her jacket.

She'd worn nothing underneath but a gold spangled bustier. Joseph had actually groaned aloud. Fortunately, the band had been playing too loudly for his date to hear.

"Enough to make every stud in Bogart's go wild."

"Including you?"

Joseph ignored that remark. "When she tossed her

jacket, she brought down the house. Next came her bangle bracelets, one by one. By now every man in the room is yelling, 'Take it off. Take it all off.' "

"Not even Maxie would go that far. Or did she?"

"She didn't. She stopped with her shoes."

When the first one had sailed through the air, there'd been a stampede to catch it. A tall, lanky man in a cowboy hat had snagged it. He immediately poured his beer into the shoe and took a long swig. Everybody had yelled like crazy.

When she'd taken off her second shoe, he had been determined to catch it, no matter who got in his way. And dozens had. Every red-blooded man in the room had vied for Maxie's second shoe. Fortunately Joseph had the long arms of a very tall man.

When he'd snatched it out of the air, Maxie had missed a beat in her song. She recovered quickly enough, but that marked the end of her striptease act.

If Joseph hadn't caught her shoe, how far would she have gone? With Maxie, you never knew. That was one of the things that made her so exciting.

"And that's how I came to have one of Maxie's shoes. End of story."

"Who do you think you're kidding? I'm your brother, remember? I've had your number since we were kids." Crash rummaged in the refrigerator and came up with fixings for ham and cheese sandwiches. "Want one?"

"Sure."

"Look, first of all you're out with that woman from the chancery clerk's office, which means you've ended it with Susan. Joe minus one." Crash didn't need confirmation. He knew his brother well.

He passed Joe a sandwich, then made one for himself. "Second, you're in a place you wouldn't have been caught dead in last week. I suspect that has something to do with Maxie, but what I don't know is how she figures in this equation."

"She doesn't. I can't think of a woman more totally unsuitable for me than Maxie Corban."

"That's what I thought about B. J. when I first met her. And look how all that turned out."

"You're not suggesting that we're alike, are you?"

"I don't know, Joe. For a minute there, I thought you'd discovered you had a heart."

"I've discovered a number of things, namely that I need a little more excitement in my life. But I've never made life-altering decisions based on messy emotions, and I don't intend to start now."

"Someday I'll remind you of that."

Joseph put the pie plates in the sink and turned on the water.

"Don't make any rash judgments because of one incident at Bogart's, Crash. I'm making a few changes in my life, that's all."

TEN

The gold shoe sat on the table between them.

"I thought you might like to have the shoe you lost," Joseph said.

"I didn't lose it," Maxie said. "I tossed it." Suddenly she began to laugh.

"What's so funny?"

"Me. You. Us. This whole situation. I suddenly had a ridiculous vision of myself as Cinderella and you as Prince Charming."

Maxie could tell by his smile that he was pleased. Puffing up his ego was the last thing in the world she wanted to do for him. She plucked the shoe off the table and tossed it into a desk drawer, then sat back down to face her opponent.

He was dressed casually, his shirt open at the neck. There was too much temptation for her. Maxie wished for his three-piece suit. Not that he didn't look good in suits, but more of him was covered.

"You got my letter," she said.

"Yes."

Obviously that's why he had come. How else could she explain Joseph Beauregard sitting in her office at the end of the day? And where was Claude when she needed him? It didn't take that long to go to the post office and fetch the mail.

"I suppose you want to talk about the party."

"I have two words to say about the party. No zebras."

"You could have said that in a note. I thought we agreed. No personal contact. Communication by courier only."

"That was your idea, not mine. Anyhow, I'm changing the rules." His smile was slow and easy. "All of them."

Maxie's heart did a somersault. For a moment she pictured herself floating across the room into Joseph's arms, pictured the two of them dancing slowly while celestial music played, pictured them settling in front of a fireplace making mad, passionate love.

She'd better pull herself together, and fast.

For one thing, her office didn't have a fireplace. For another, she wasn't about to make a fool of herself over a man who ditched his fiancée and immediately squired a woman completely opposite to her out for a night on the town.

She was still steaming over the two of them at Bogart's, cuddled into a cozy corner. Not that she wanted him for herself, of course. He was off-limits.

"Obviously," she said.

His grin was wicked. "You're referring, of course, to last night."

"Off with the old, on with the new. Or used, as the case may be."

"The cat has claws."

"Watch out or you might get scratched."

"I can't wait."

Maxie didn't know what to think about this turn of events. She'd never met a man who was so many different people, all rolled into one. And every single one of them fascinated her.

Still, she was cautious. Her track record was atrocious, her history with Joseph, appalling. Besides all that, there was her sister to think of.

Still, Joseph tugged at her heart in a way no man ever had. If he kept on sitting in her office looking delicious, she'd do something foolish.

She deliberately looked at her watch. Under ordinary circumstances she would never be so rude, but these were extraordinary circumstances.

"If you have nothing else to say about the party, I *do* have work to do."

"I didn't come to see you about the baby's party. I came on business."

"What kind of business?"

She regretted her words the minute they were out of her mouth.

"What did you have in mind, Maxie?"

He grinned wickedly. She kept a careful rein on her tart tongue.

"Interior design, of course. After all, I am Magic Maxie."

"You're magic, all right."

He pulled out his pipe and tamped in tobacco, eyeing her over the bowl. If he hoped for a reaction from her, she planned to disappoint him.

"You said you came on business."

"Yes. I want to hire you to redecorate my master suite."

"In your office?"

"No. In my home. My bedroom."

She couldn't think of a worse situation, cooped up all day with his personal belongings. His shirts and ties. His socks and shorts. She wondered whether he wore briefs or boxers. Probably boxers. She'd never trusted a man who wore boxers.

"We're happy to have you as a client."

Glad for the opportunity to move farther away, she went to her desk and thumbed through her appointment book.

"We'll need to consult you from time to time, of course. I'm on a job right now, but I can make your first appointment with Claude sometime next week. Is that satisfactory?"

"No."

"No?"

"I want you."

The emphasis he put on the words made her hot all over.

"I'm afraid that's impossible."

"Then we don't have a deal." He stood up. "I want only you."

She felt a hot flush creep into her face. Was he doing that deliberately?

"With the party coming up and the job I'm on . . ."

"You can do the job whenever you're free. I don't need to consult you." He tossed his house key onto the table. "You have carte blanche."

It was a dream job. And an opportunity too good to resist.

"You're sure about that?" She suppressed her grin.

"Absolutely. I know you're good."

His face lit with devilment. Was he toying with her again?

"Decorate the suite as if it were your own. I'll pay for whatever you do."

"All right, then. I'll do the job. I have only one stipulation. Once I start, you can't come into the suite."

"No problem. I'll move my things into one of the other bedrooms. Just let me know when."

"I think I can reshuffle my schedule and start tomorrow."

She didn't offer to shake hands, and neither did he. After the door closed behind him, Maxie began to laugh.

Any man who would leave her tumbled on the sofa because of a fiancée then turn up a few nights later with another woman deserved whatever he got.

"You'll pay, all right."

She raced to her supply closet and dragged out a wad of fabric swatches.

"Good Lord." Claude stood in the middle of the office, with one hand clutching the mail and the other clutching his heart. "What *is* it?"

Maxie held up the swatch of fabric. "What do you think?"

"I think it deserves its own cage or else a decent burial."

"Perfect. That's what I think too." She set it aside, then jotted notes.

"You're not planning on *using* that?"

"I am."

Humming, Maxie flipped open a catalog and began to circle items. Curious, Claude peered over her shoulder.

"Is that what I think it is?"

"Yes."

"You're not serious? . . . You *are* serious. Good Lord, I've got to have tea."

"Fix me a cup too."

He heaped them both with sugar and came back to the table so he could look over her shoulder. Every time she circled an item he gasped.

"Maxie, what kind of job is this?"

"Revenge."

ELEVEN

It wasn't fair that the scent of Joseph's aftershave lingered in his bedroom. It wasn't fair that he'd left his robe hanging on the bathroom door or that his damp towel was still in the shower stall.

"Maxie, get a grip," she told herself.

She was not there to drive herself crazy with wild, impossible dreams, she was there for revenge.

The first thing that had to go was the bedding. Maxie pulled the green comforter off and piled it in the middle of the floor. She had no illusions about what she was doing. She was ridding the bedroom of everything his fiancée had touched. She didn't plan to leave a single reminder of the oh-so-correct Susan.

With the spread off, she placed the swatch of leopard-print velour on his sheets. It gave exactly the touch she had in mind. Let him romp with his latest conquest on that.

Her conscience pricked her only slightly as she

picked up the bedside phone and placed an order for the custom-made comforter.

"You want to cat around, Joseph Beauregard? Never fear, Magic Maxie is here. I'll create a lair worthy of your newfound talents."

She turned on the radio, found a station that played lively music to her liking, then immersed herself in her decorating task.

Joseph knew when he let himself in the front door that Maxie was in his house. He'd thought of nothing else all day.

When he hung up his jacket, he caught sight of something bright red. Her sweater was hanging in his closet.

He went toward the kitchen, intending to make himself a snack, then settle into his den with the *Wall Street Journal*. Music drifted down the staircase, something lively. He knew the tune but not the words.

Joseph started humming, his feet started tapping, and before you could blink an eye he bounded up the stairs, two at a time. Maxie was singing along with the radio.

He stood in the hallway, listening. Now he knew why the tune was so familiar. Judy Garland had sung it in *A Star Is Born*—"Lose That Long Face."

It was impossible not to smile. Joseph realized he'd been doing a lot of that lately, especially today while he'd sat at his desk picturing Maxie in his house.

What was she doing in there? Whatever it was, she

was having fun. Would she put touches of red in his bedroom? Something purple? Perhaps a throw pillow.

With his hand on the knob, he paused. She'd given specific instructions. He was not to enter his suite until she'd finished the job.

Instead, he knocked on the door.

There was silence, then Maxie called, "Who is it?"

"Joe."

"Joe?" The door opened a crack. He saw a pert nose, the brightest blue eyes this side of heaven, tousled red hair, and fingernails painted yellow. They looked like sunshine.

"You're home." She glanced at her watch. "I didn't expect you."

"I took off early today. I knew you'd be here decorating."

"You can't come in. I want to surprise you."

Warmth flooded through him. He couldn't remember ever being with a woman who cared enough about him to want to surprise him.

"Why are you here?" she said.

"I live here."

"I mean, at this door."

From long practice, Joe knew how to think on his feet. "I forgot to get my handkerchiefs."

"I'll get them for you. Where are they?"

"Top drawer of the antique chest."

With his ear pressed against the door, he unabashedly eavesdropped. She opened the drawer, then silence. Then he heard her say something. Pressing closer to the door, he deciphered the words.

"Damn, damn damn," she said. "Jockeys, size thirty-four."

Two spots of bright pink colored her cheeks when she opened the door.

"Here." She thrust the handkerchiefs through the crack, then tried to slam the door.

"Wait." Now what? All Joseph knew was that he couldn't let her go back behind the closed door. "Do you want some pie? It's lemon icebox."

"Hmmm."

She flicked the tip of her tongue over her bottom lip. It was one of the most erotic gestures Joe had ever seen. That small movement, combined with the delicious love-sound she'd made excited him more than all his former fiancée's foreplay.

Daily he saw fresh evidence that he'd done the right thing.

"I have lemonade," he said. "To cool us off."

"Lemonade?" She brushed a damp lock of hair off her forehead. "I really shouldn't. I have work to do."

"It won't take long."

"All right. Even slaves need breaks. I'll just have a quickie."

If she had any experience reading a man's eyes, she'd know beyond a shadow of a doubt what he wanted to do: He wanted to bend her lush body to his and enter her with a thrust that lifted her feet off the ground. He wanted to release her ripe breasts from the wisp of black lace he'd glimpsed, then suckle until she was writhing and moaning. He wanted to spend the rest of the afternoon in a slow tango of love.

And when it was over, when he'd taken the edge off his hunger, he wanted to carry her to his king-size bed, wrap his arms around her, and sleep until desire spurred him awake. Then he wanted to start with her, all over again.

He could tell by her expression that she knew exactly what he was thinking. What he couldn't tell was whether or not she liked it.

"Close your eyes," she said.

"Why? Don't you like what you see in them?"

Her pink tongue appeared once more, briefly, leaving her bottom lip wet and slick and kissable.

"I don't want you to see inside when I come out." Obediently he closed his eyes. "I'll tell you when to open them." He heard the click of the door. "All right. You can open them now."

Maxie took his breath away. Up close she was delicious, flushed skin and dewy lips. Bangles sparkled on her arms, a tiered denim skirt swayed around her legs, and a white peasant blouse slid off one shoulder.

"I'm starved," she said.

"Me too." He devoured her with his eyes.

"Shall we eat?"

"I'd like nothing better."

Riveted, they stood in the hall, body heat rising between them, eyes locked, hips swaying. He couldn't keep his hands off her.

Her skin was like silk. He slid his fingers over her scented skin, down her neck, and across her bare shoulder. Maxie sucked in a sharp breath.

His eyes never leaving hers, Joe bent down and

traced the path with his lips. One touch was not enough. One taste only whetted his appetite for more.

"Joe . . ."

Her voice issued a warning, but her eyes issued an invitation. He accepted.

He crushed her hard against his body, bent swiftly, and captured her lips. She responded with an eagerness that took his breath away. Theirs was not the soft experimental kiss of strangers but the deep, hungry kiss of lovers.

Her lips were wet, open, wild. He plunged his tongue inside, lapping up her delicious juices, exploring her soft recesses. She made delirious love-sounds.

Joe felt as if he were going to explode. Bracing her against the wall, he thrust with tongue and hips in a rhythm as old as time. Her skirt swayed around them. Her fragrance invaded his already heightened senses, spurring him on.

"You drive me crazy," he said.

Maxie stiffened. She couldn't believe what she was doing. And in Joseph's own house.

Only the day before she'd sworn to herself that he was definitely off-limits, and there she was acting like an alley cat. And all because she'd discovered Jockey shorts in his chest of drawers.

That wasn't the whole reason she was backed against the wall panting, of course, but it was a big part of it.

She shoved against his chest.

"Fortunately, you don't have the same effect on me."

If he looked puzzled, she supposed he had every right, but she wasn't about to let that stop her.

"If this is your idea of hospitality, it stinks."

B. J. would be so proud of her. Head high, she marched down the stairs, chattering all the way. Besides humming, it was what she did when she was nervous.

"I've changed my mind about pie. It's probably laced with aphrodisiacs." Joe didn't say a word. Good. Let him listen. He might learn a thing or two. "I wonder if your ex-fiancée knows how lucky she is. Honestly, you have the habits of a tomcat. Whoever happens to be in the alley, that's the pussycat you want."

He roared with laughter. Bounding down the stairs, he caught her arm and drew her up short.

"What's so darned funny?"

"I enjoyed that performance tremendously, Maxie. Are you always this passionate about everything you do?"

"Sometimes I throw things." She tried to shake him off. "Let go of me."

He ignored her. "I wouldn't call you a pussycat. I think wildcat is more like it."

"You bring out the beast in me." It was the wrong thing to say.

"The same here, Maxie." He undressed her with his eyes. "You definitely bring out the animal in me."

She lifted her hair off her hot neck. She felt as if she'd been in a steam bath.

"That's not the kind of beast I'm talking about."

"You could have fooled me."

She didn't know why she'd ever gotten into a contest of words with a lawyer. She knew from experience that you could never win. B. J. had always outtalked, outfoxed, and outmaneuvered her, even when they were children.

At the foot of the stairs, Joseph steered her toward the kitchen. Lord, she'd never known that merely walking beside a man could be so erotic. She felt like one of the Salem witches, staked out with fire licking up her legs.

"I'd like that lemonade now," she said.

He poured in silence, set the glasses on the table, then pulled out a chair for her. She'd have thought he was a perfect gentleman if she didn't know better.

"I'll have mine upstairs." She jerked up her glass and was on the way out the door when he stopped her.

"Why are you afraid of me, Maxie?"

It was the sort of challenge she couldn't resist.

"I'm not afraid of the devil," she said.

"Every time I kiss you, you run like hell. I know it's not displeasure, because you kiss me back." She'd opened her mouth to argue, but he didn't give her time. "That leaves only one alternative: fear."

Unconsciously she put the cool glass to her hot neck.

"Don't you dare slide that glass down the neck of your blouse. I'm only human, you know."

"Is that why you back me into the first piece of furniture you can find every time you see me?"

"I know it's not a gentlemanly thing to do. It's

hardly even civil. What can I say, Maxie? You're irresistible."

She slugged her drink, then plopped the glass back onto the table.

"I don't know why I'm doing this," she muttered.

"You said you were thirsty." He assessed the level of the glass. "From the way you slugged it down, you were."

"I'm not talking about lemonade."

"I'm lost. Enlighten me."

"All right, you asked a question, and here's your answer: I only have the knack for long-distance relationships." He quirked an eyebrow. "That's right. The telephone."

He had the good grace to be slightly embarrassed.

"To be honest with you, I don't have the knack for relationships, either. Especially with you."

"Because I'm so inappropriate?"

"Maxie, you'll have to admit that we're totally unsuitable for each other."

"If I cared about suitability, I would. Fortunately, I don't give a fig for suitability and convention and public opinion."

"What do you care about, Maxie?"

"Family. B. J. and Crash and the baby. I'm not about to do anything to mess that up."

She marched out of the kitchen, head high, gloating that she'd had the last word.

Upstairs she locked herself into his bedroom, then raced to the mirror. She looked like a shipwreck. She pinched her cheeks to give them color. Why hadn't she worn a brighter blouse? Anything except a white one, which made her look like a bar of Ivory soap.

She groaned and plopped onto the middle of his bed. Why couldn't she have met him somewhere out of state or even out of town? Why did he have to be B. J.'s brother-in-law?

The scent of a woodsy aftershave surrounded her. Flopping over, she buried her head in Joe's pillow and inhaled. Her body reacted immediately.

Hugging his pillow, she actually fantasized. When she had to clamp her knees together and bite her tongue to keep from groaning, she threw the pillow from her and scrambled off the bed.

Good Lord, she was turning into a ridiculous woman. What did she care if she looked like a bar of colorless soap to Joseph Beauregard? She was in his house to do a decorating job, not to seduce him.

Maxie attacked the curtains next. As she measured the windows she was thinking about the glamorous jungle-print silk blouse in her closet. She would wear that tomorrow. After all, it never hurt to look nice on the job.

TWELVE

At ten-thirty that night Maxie's phone rang. She muted the TV and picked it up.

"Don't hang up, Maxie." It was Joseph.

"I can't. You're a client."

"I'm not calling as a client, I'm calling as a telephone lover."

"If this is your idea of a sick joke, it's not funny."

"This is no joke, Maxie. I've been thinking about our conversation in the kitchen, and I've come to the conclusion that a telephone relationship is exactly what we need."

"I don't need anything from you."

"Are you sure about that? . . . Remember the kiss upstairs? Didn't it make you want more, Maxie?"

"Yes. . . . Why are you doing this, Joe? To torture me?"

"No. You said you were good at long-distance relationships, and I admitted that I'm not good at any kind

106

of relationship. Furthermore, since we've both admitted that we're wrong for each other but it's perfectly obvious we can't keep our hands off each other, a telephone liaison is the perfect solution. Don't you agree?"

"No. *No* relationship is the perfect solution."

"Then I suppose I'll continue to turn up accidentally when you're in my house, and you'll continue to fondle my underwear behind closed doors."

"I did not fondle your underwear."

"Jockeys, size thirty-four."

"All right. Maybe I did pick them up and look. But only out of curiosity."

"Curiosity killed the cat."

"I'm no cat."

"Yes, you are, Maxie. A wildcat. And I can hear you purring."

It was true. Joseph had an incredibly sexy telephone voice, and she'd already slid down in her chair. She was purring and was on the verge of moaning.

Maybe he was right. What would be wrong with a telephone relationship? Nice and safe. Keep the distance and nobody would be hurt.

She hadn't had any relationship for so long, she was in danger of turning into a prune.

"Here are the rules," she said. "The relationship will be confined strictly to the phone. We have as little personal contact as possible, and when we do, we're merely nodding acquaintances. We make no attempts to cross over the boundaries. Agreed?"

"Up to a point."

"Up to what point?"

"If either of us decides we want more, we have to be honest. No pretending."

"I thought we already agreed that we're wrong for each other."

"That's a given, Maxie. But I can't predict the future. Can you?"

"I can't predict the future, but I can tell you my decision, and it won't change: You're strictly off-limits, Joe. Except on the telephone, of course. Long-distance, there are no holds barred."

"No holes barred? Intriguing."

"You're shameless."

"I'm also hot. Are you hot, Maxie?"

"Yes."

"Tell me how much."

"My face is flushed and my legs are quivering."

"Good. Pretend that I'm touching you. My hands are on you, Maxie. You like that, don't you?"

"You know I do."

"How do you want to be touched? Tell me."

"Gently. Like a kiss."

"Do it, Maxie, but imagine it's me."

"This is wicked . . . decadent . . ."

"And altogether delicious. I want a taste. My lips are on you. Do you feel my mouth?"

"Yes."

"How does it feel?"

"Wonderful."

"Touch me, Maxie. Wrap your hand around me. Feel that? Feel what you do for me?"

"I want it, Joe."

"How do you want it?"

"Here . . . now . . ."

Maxie was almost incoherent with need. She'd always been the aggressive one in her telephone relationships, the one who took the lead. No man had ever been as bold as Joseph, so wicked, so daring.

"Here it is, Maxie. Do you feel that? Do you feel how well we fit together?"

With her mind she brought Joseph into her house, into her living room, into her body. She closed her eyes and he was there, parting her thighs, burying himself deep with one smooth thrust. She lost her breath.

"Slow and easy, Maxie. Take it slow and easy."

"Oh, God, I can't . . . I want it all . . . now, Joe . . . now."

She gathered force like a tornado, building and building until the first spontaneous explosion hit. She cried out her pleasure, then held on to the receiver, panting.

"I'm not done with you yet. Come here, feel how I still want you?" She managed a strangled murmur. "I'm stretching out on the floor. Slide over me, slowly . . . slow . . . ly. That's it."

She felt the pressure build once more, felt the tightening of her muscles, the heaviness of her breasts.

Joe talked her through, and her imagination did the rest. She cried out again and again, then lay against the chair cushions, limp, barely able to cling to the receiver.

"Good night, Magic Maxie. Till we talk again."

She pressed her lips to the receiver, then sat listening to the dial tone, too languid to hang up.

"You look like the cat that swallowed the canary." Claude checked his watch. "And you're late."

"Only fifteen minutes, Claude." Maxie dropped her briefcase on the sofa and headed to the coffeepot. "I hope you made it strong today."

She poured herself a cup.

"Why? The new job getting to you or something?"

"Or something."

"Okay. Be that way. Don't tell me what new madness you've gotten yourself into."

"How do you know I've gotten into some new madness?"

"Because you wouldn't be Maxie if you hadn't. And you never did answer my question about the Beauregard job. How's it going?"

"That depends on your point of view. Great, if I stick with my original plan. Lousy, if I decide to start over and make the Beauregard lair a showplace worthy of *Architectural Digest.*" She sipped her coffee. "I think I'll start over."

"Hmmm. Intriguing." Claude perched on the edge of the desk and riffled through the mail. "He was at Bogart's again last night."

"Joseph?" Maxie had to sit down.

"Who else are we talking about? He was with a different woman. Some cheesy brunette."

"Susan?"

"Definitely not Susan. Do you know that little number at the bank who messed up our deposit once? She was the one. They left early. It doesn't take a genius to figure out why."

Fury propelled Maxie from the sofa. So that was why Joseph had called her. He'd been all hot and bothered and his little banker friend had ditched him.

Or maybe he was merely putting notches on his new belt.

She couldn't wait to get to Joseph's house. The mirrored ceiling came next. She poured her coffee out, jerked up her briefcase, and stalked toward the door.

"Maxie, wait. There was a phone call for you before you came in."

"Who?" If he said it was Joseph, she was going to hit something.

"Your sister. She wants you to come over to her house for dinner tomorrow night."

She'd be willing to bet Joseph would be there too.

"Call her back and tell her I'll be there, with bells on."

The first thing she did when she got to the Beauregard mansion was strip off her leopard-print silk blouse. She'd work naked before she'd be caught dressed up for Tupelo's newest stud. Anyhow, who would see her?

She hung her blouse in Joseph's closet, then immersed herself in work. The sound of the vacuum cleaner brought her back to the real world.

Joseph? Surely not. She jerked open his chest of drawers and pulled on one of his T-shirts.

At noon hunger drove her out of the room. It was in the kitchen that she met Hazel.

"You're redoing Mr. B's bedroom?" Hazel beamed. "I hope you get rid of those ugly brown curtains."

"Oh, I'll get rid of them, all right, and everything else that doesn't suit his new lifestyle." Feeling sneaky and downright mean, Maxie perched on a bar stool with her ham sandwich and tried to look innocent. "Now . . . tell me what the *real* Mr. B is like."

"He'd like to have you think he's a stick-in-the-mud, but he sleeps naked."

Maxie was taken aback. Somehow she'd never have dreamed Hazel was his type.

Hazel laughed. "Oh, lordy. Wait till I tell my sister."

"What?"

"It's written all over your face. You think I'm one of his new girlfriends."

"Well, you never know."

"He leaves his pajamas folded on the chair, but I know they've never been slept in. They're silk, and silk wrinkles when you use it." Hazel chuckled. "See. It's that simple." She hung up her dish towel. "He's a good man, my Mr. B."

Maxie lost her appetite. "You know what, Hazel, I

ought to be flayed with a wet noodle. I have no business asking you nosy questions about your employer."

"That's all right, Maxie. I would never tell you anything I thought might do him harm. I love Mr. B. But you know, I can't say I was all that upset when he broke up with Miss Susan. She's a little too uppity for me."

"You won't tell him I asked about him?"

"Nary a word, child. You just go back upstairs and fix Mr. B up."

"I will. That's a promise."

THIRTEEN

Maxie was tucked into bed reading a book when the phone rang. She glanced at the clock. Eleven. Only a telephone lover would call that late.

She started to let the phone ring, then changed her mind.

"Are you in bed, Maxie?"

As usual, the mere sound of Joseph's voice sent shivers over her.

"Yes. I'm reading a good book."

"What are you wearing?"

"Baby doll pajamas, pink with red hearts."

"Sounds delicious. I'd like to taste your hearts, Maxie. All of them."

His voice seduced, and Maxie fought against being spellbound. She thought of all the women he was squiring around town and pure jealousy raged through her. Not that she had any right to complain. By its very nature, a telephone relationship wasn't usually exclusive. To be fair, she and Joe had never agreed that their relationship would be anything more than a convenience, a safe way to vent the passion that always simmered between them.

Still, she didn't want him to think she was the kind of woman who could be picked up then cast off like an old pair of shoes. He thought she was inappropriate: Let him add inconvenient to the list.

"I'm reading a thriller," she said, "and I've practically scared myself to death. I'm not in the mood for sweet talk."

"Do you read a lot, Maxie?"

"Yes, mostly fiction of all kinds, but sometimes I love to plow into a big fat volume of nonfiction, particularly if it's about World War Two."

"That's amazing. I'm a history buff, too, particularly of that era. They had the best music, the best clothes, the best war. Have you read *Patton: A Genius for War*?"

"I read it and loved it. Patton makes a convincing case for reincarnation."

"That's exactly what I was thinking."

Maxie could hear the smile in Joe's voice. She made a comfortable nest of her covers and sat cross-legged, smiling.

"Do you eat popcorn in bed, Joe?"

"With butter?"

"Dripping."

It didn't take much to trigger Joseph's libido. He made a low sound, half growl, half moan.

"That's the way I love it," he said. "But I prefer

eating it in front of a cozy fire late at night with the grandfather clock ticking and the moon riding the tops of the trees."

"That's poetic." As well as erotic, but Maxie kept that to herself. "I didn't know you had a lyrical turn of mind."

"I have two spiral-bound notebooks filled with poetry on the top shelf of my closet, but it's a deep, dark secret."

"I love discovering secrets. Do you have more?"

"Yes."

"You're being cagey."

"If you want to know my secrets, you have to pay for them, Maxie. Are you willing to pay?"

"That depends on the price."

"Negotiable. For instance, I'll tell you one secret, and you have to remove one item of clothing, your choice."

With them it always came back to desire. Excitement sizzled through Maxie, and she shoved aside her covers.

"It's a deal," she said.

"Take something off, Maxie. . . . What did you remove?"

"My pajama top."

"Do you sleep in a bra or are you naked underneath?"

"Naked."

"That's good, Maxie. I'm naked too. I fold my pajamas and leave them on a chair so Hazel won't know, but I sleep naked."

Telling him she already knew that secret would be a betrayal of Hazel. Maxie kept it to herself.

"Take something else off," he commanded. "What was it this time?"

"Socks." She giggled.

"Socks?"

"Sometimes my feet get cold, and I wear socks to bed."

"If I were in your bed you wouldn't need socks. I'd warm you up, Maxie."

She got caught up in the image of Joseph spread across her bed. It was an old-fashioned iron bedstead, painted white, that had belonged to her grandmother. Big man that he was, Joe would crowd her in the bed. They'd have to sleep close. She loved the idea of sleeping close.

Before she'd discovered she had no talent for relationships, she used to imagine herself married and snuggled close, spoon fashion, a man's arms around her, her back pressed close to his chest.

She sighed.

"Did you say something, Maxie?"

"I was just clearing my throat. . . . What you said does not qualify as a secret. I strip, you tell. That's the bargain."

"All right. Here it is: I have a mole on my left hip."

"What kind? How is it shaped?"

Joseph chuckled. "I think I'll save that secret for another time . . . perhaps when you're in my bed and can see for yourself."

"People in telephone relationships don't get in each other's beds. We agreed."

He did the worst thing a man can do to a woman: He didn't respond. There was a long maddening silence. She wasn't about to give him the satisfaction of pressing the issue.

"Maxie, are you still there?"

"I'm here."

"Here's your secret: I'm superstitious about black cats. Are you ready for another?"

"Yes."

"Then take something off. . . . What will it be, Maxie?"

"My pajama bottoms."

"Are you wearing anything underneath?"

"No."

"Remove them slowly, Maxie. Let your hands glide along your skin as you peel them down your legs. Pretend they're my hands."

Heat flooded her. "I thought this game was about secrets."

"It is, Maxie. . . . Are you caressing your legs?"

"I am." She made no attempt to disguise her breathlessness. After all, this was only a game.

"Tell me when they're off."

"Now."

"Good. Now lie back on the pillows, Maxie, nice and easy." She didn't argue. "Spread your hair across the pillow. Is the pillowcase white?"

"Yes. With a lace edge."

"Is the bedside lamp on?"

"How did you know?"

"You were reading. . . . Now, Maxie, lie very still with the lamplight shining on your hair. Are you obeying me?"

"Yes."

"Good. Then here's my secret: I fantasize about you. I picture you lying just that way, your hair like flame, your legs parted. And then I picture myself bending down to taste you, my lips closing around you, my tongue delving inside. I imagine that you taste like some exotic fruit, passion fruit perhaps, with just a hint of cream."

She clamped her lower lip between her teeth to bite back the spontaneous orgasm, but there was no holding back, and no way to disguise it.

There was a long silence at the other end of the line. All Maxie could hear was the sound of heavy breathing. Limp, she lay against the covers, her eyes closed, her lips pressed close to the receiver. Finally Joe broke the silence.

"You do the same thing to me. 'Night, Maxie."

He'd hung up before she could muster up the energy to say good night. She traced a finger around the rim of the receiver.

" 'Night, Joe."

She made kissing noises toward the receiver as she hung up. Then she lay back against her pillows and wondered why this telephone relationship felt different from the others, why it felt more intimate, more satisfying.

She switched off the light, then pulled the covers up to her chin.

"This is a dangerous game you're playing, Maxie," she said.

Joe arrived at the farm thirty minutes early so he could be there when Maxie arrived. He had studiously avoided showing up at his house while she was still there working. Though not seeing each other was part of their bargain, he was foolishly excited about the prospect of seeing her tonight.

His brother was so excited about his newborn son that he didn't even notice the time.

"Come on in here, Uncle, and see the finest little boy God ever put on this earth." Crash proudly showed off his rosy-faced son sleeping in his crib. "Feel that little fist close around your finger? He's strong as an ox."

He'd never seen any creature so fragile-looking, but he didn't contradict his brother.

"Here. Do you want to hold him?"

Without waiting for confirmation, Crash scooped the baby up and arranged him in Joe's arms. Joe was terrified.

"What if he wakes up? What if I don't hold him right? What if he gets hungry?"

Crash laughed. "You've got a lot to learn about babies."

"I don't know that it's necessary to learn."

"Someday you'll be having one of your own."

"I'm in no danger at the moment."

The baby stirred and opened his eyes. It took him a while to focus, but when he did, he looked straight up at his uncle. Joe fell in love on the spot.

"Would you just look at that? He smiled at me."

"See. Didn't I tell you he's a genius? Most babies that young don't smile, but my son's got them all beat."

Enchanted, Joe bent close to his nephew's tiny face and did what besotted grown-ups around the world do with babies: He began to croon baby talk.

"How's my widdle wascal? Can you give me a widdle smile? Can you smile for Unca Joe?" He looked up, beaming. "He smiled at me again."

"He's smiling because his aunt Maxie is here."

She entered the room like a parade, jangle bracelets tinkling, skirt swirling, eyes flashing, hair bouncing. Joe wasn't prepared for her impact. When a man and woman have been intimate, even on the phone, they are connected in ways that defy description. Every cell in his body cried out for her, every bone, every sinew. His skin felt hot and tight, as if he'd grown too big for it.

Crash and the baby faded into the background, and all he could see was Maxie, vivid in red, crooning as she moved his way.

"There's my little nephew. There's my big boy. Can I hold him?"

"Be sure to support his head," Joe said. "And hold him close so your body heat keeps him warm."

"If you can do it, I can."

When she took the baby, she made as little contact with Joe as possible, a mere brush of fingertips against his own, a slight swish of skirt against his trousers, a whisper touch of her long hair as she bent over the tiny bundle. She retreated quickly to the other side of the room.

"Maxie . . ."

She warned him with her eyes. Playing by the rules had never been so hard.

"Don't you gentlemen have something to do around the grill? Baby Joe and I are going to find his mommy."

"She's in the bedroom trying to find a skirt that will zip," Crash said. "I'd tread lightly if I were you."

"Thanks for the warning." Without a backward glance, Maxie was gone.

"Whew," Crash said. "Does it feel cooler in here to you?"

"At least ten degrees." Joe was hardly one to judge. Every time he came near Maxie he heated up.

"Man, I've never seen her like that. What did you do to make her so mad, Joe?"

"Who, me?"

"Don't give me that."

"Give you what?"

"You always answer a question with another question when you're being cagey."

"I'm not being cagey. Who knows what makes any woman tick, especially one as unpredictable as Maxie Corban."

"Look, Joe, I know you and she don't see eye to

eye about the baby's party, but try to keep things as civil as possible tonight. I don't want B. J. to be upset."

"You don't have a thing to worry about. I'll be a perfect gentleman with Maxie."

"What else would I expect from you? I don't know why I even said anything. Nerves, I guess." He clapped his brother on the shoulder. "Let's go to the grill. You be the gentleman and I'll be the trouble-maker, as usual."

Outside Joseph could see Maxie silhouetted through the window. He thought of all the ways they'd been intimate via telephone, and suddenly the telephone relationship struck him as an act of coward-ice. What if he *had* failed with Susan? That didn't necessarily mean he was destined to fail with every woman.

Not that his track record lately was anything to brag about. He'd bored Letty stiff, and vice versa. The girl from the bank had chattered about nail polish and hairdos for two hours, and by the time he got home he'd had to take two aspirin for the pain. Only a phone call to Maxie saved his sanity.

Maybe he just wasn't cut out to have a relationship. Maybe, after all, the telephone was his best bet.

Still, being a gentleman around Maxie this evening was going to be one of the hardest things he'd ever done.

"Who's chasing you? The devil?" B. J. was trying to button a chambray skirt around her thickened waist.

"You might say that." Holding her precious bundle close, Maxie negotiated her way across B. J.'s bedroom as if it were a minefield. When she got to the rocking chair, she breathed a sigh of relief. "Good grief. I didn't know having babies was so much work."

"It's only work if you're terrified. Relax, Maxie. He's just a little thing. He won't bite."

"What if he wets?"

"Then you'll have the privilege of changing his diaper."

Maxie rocked the baby and sang a lullaby she remembered from their childhood. Outside, Crash and Joe were laughing at something one of them had said. She could see them, two big, handsome men, swathed in aprons, pushing hamburgers around on the grill.

"B. J. . . . What's it like to be married?"

"Strawberry shortcake."

"Be serious."

"I am. You know how the first strawberries taste, fresh and juicy and full of a sweetness you can't describe, and then you add a dollop of whipped cream and pile it all on top of a good hunk of yellow butter cake and you've got heaven."

"I think I'm going to cry."

"Here, use my handkerchief. I hardly ever need them anymore." Maxie sniffed into her sister's handkerchief. "What's this all about, anyhow?"

"I don't know. Maybe I'm jealous. Suddenly you have everything and my life seems so dull by comparison."

"Pooh. You don't have a jealous bone in your

body. . . . This skirt's not going to button." B. J. pulled a loose jumper over her head, then took her baby. "Come on, punkin, dinnertime." She sat on the edge of the bed with the baby cuddled close.

Maxie blew her nose. How was she ever going to have a baby if she couldn't even let a man get close?

"One thing's for sure," she said. "I can't do it over the telephone."

"Do what?"

"Get pregnant."

"Maxie, you are in a mood. Have you met somebody I don't know about?"

"No."

It was the truth. B. J. knew Joe almost as well as she knew her own husband. After all, they were family.

"Do you know something, B. J. I'm not very hungry tonight. I think I'll just go on home. I'm starting a new job next week, and I need to work on the plans."

"Maxie, I don't know what's going on, and it looks like you're not planning to tell me, but we're your family. If something's troubling you, the best thing to do is stay for dinner. If anybody can cheer you up, it's Crash."

B. J. didn't try to manipulate her with guilt, but Maxie felt guilty anyway.

"I'm selfish to the bone." She sat on the edge of the bed and watched as her nephew wrapped his tiny hand around her finger. "This is your big night, and here I am acting like a baby. I'm staying."

"I'm glad."

B. J. and Crash were obviously in love. They sat close, leaning toward each other frequently for a touch, a secret smile, a kiss. Joseph wondered how this brother of his, in love with long distances and a Harley, had managed to make the giant leap required to settle into marriage and fatherhood. Joseph had always been the Beauregard considered most likely to domesticate, the one who would settle into marriage early and present a child destined to carry out the Beauregard tradition of being a lawyer.

He wasn't even close to marriage, let alone fatherhood. And at the rate he was going, that would never happen. As he reached for the ketchup his arm brushed against Maxie's.

"Excuse me," he said, withdrawing quickly, electrified.

"Certainly."

She leaned over the table to retrieve the mustard, and the hem of her skirt touched his thigh. Was she naked underneath? At that moment he'd give everything he owned for the right to slide his hand under her skirt and discover the truth for himself.

When she sank back into her chair, her leg brushed against his.

"Pardon me," she said.

"Of course."

Crash and B. J. exchanged a knowing look. Joseph wasn't about to do anything that would trigger a later cross-examination by his brother. One thing was certain: He couldn't spend the rest of the evening pretending that Maxie was nothing more to him than a mere acquaintance.

He glanced at his watch. "I hate to be a party pooper, but I have to get back to the office."

"Do you really have to leave so early?"

"Sorry, B. J. Big case in court tomorrow."

"Crash . . . Maxie . . . Can't you do something?"

"You're going to miss dessert," Crash said. "Strawberry shortcake."

"Sorry, bro. Gotta go."

Joseph stood up. He was already headed toward the door when Maxie's voice stopped him.

"You're going to miss my famous tale."

His arousal was instant. Turning slowly, he smiled at her.

"Maxie, there's nothing I'd like better than to partake of your famous tail."

Heck, he thought, as he walked back to the table. Let Crash question him. He was a master of evasion.

He sat down at the table once more, deliberately pulling his chair too close to Maxie's. She sucked in a sharp breath when he pressed his knee against hers.

"Now," he said, leaning close and smiling directly into her eyes. "Where is that famous tail you're so hot to share with me?"

FOURTEEN

Maxie often regretted words spoken in haste. This was no exception. Joseph Beauregard had been in full retreat. Pure insanity had made her call him back. All her other motives were impure, every last one of them.

And now he was sitting too close, and she was casting around in her mind for a hilarious story. It didn't even have to be hilarious. A halfway funny one would do. Anything to get her off the hook. Anything to get her out of this chair, out of this room, and safe at home where she could climb into bed and lie with heart pounding and blood pumping, waiting for the phone to ring. Hoping it would and praying it wouldn't.

Propping her elbows on the table, she leaned toward her brother-in-law.

"Did I ever tell you how Magic Maxie's came into being?"

"Not that I recall."

B. J. put a hand on her husband's arm. "Darling, if you had heard this story, you'd recall it. Believe me. . . . Tell it, Maxie."

"It all started in Atlanta." Tingling all over, she was vividly aware of Joseph's intent regard. "I met Claude when I started work for Werner's Designs. He was extraordinarily talented, witty, and perfectly miserable, married to a girl named Betty, trying to be something he was not."

Joseph shifted, his leg pressed closer. Maxie felt faint.

"Werner's was a terrible place to work. The boss was a jerk, the clients were snobs, and political correctness was just beginning to rear its ugly head in the workplace."

Joe was making her so hot that Maxie had to take a long drink of iced tea to cool off. She lifted the cool glass toward the front of her blouse when she caught Joe's eye.

Her hand stopped in midair, and ice cubes clinked against glass as she set it back on the table.

"Politically correct policies were adopted right and left. I broke every rule."

"I would expect nothing less of you, Maxie," Joseph said. "You like nothing better than breaking the rules."

"How do you know?" She was still striving to preserve their image as casual acquaintances.

"B. J. tells me so."

He reached under the table and ran his hand down

the length of her leg. Smiling across the table at Crash and B. J., she nudged his hand away. He put it right back, this time underneath her skirt.

Crash and B. J. were watching her expectantly. Smiling at them, she nudged Joe's hand. He didn't budge. There was nothing to do except finish her story. Fast.

"At first Claude put notes in my box, cheering me on, then one day he joined in my insurrection. Big time."

Joe made erotic little circles on her bare knee. She galloped toward the end of her story like a racehorse sprinting for the finish line at the Kentucky Derby.

"We'd just endured a tedious workshop on sexual harassment at the workplace. Our company was going to be so politically correct that we couldn't comment on each other's clothes, let alone bodies. The moderators held up Claude's recent comment to Donna the bookkeeper as an example of what not to say in the workplace."

"What was the comment?" Crash asked.

" 'Hey, darling, you look great. Lost weight?' "

B. J. and Crash and Joe all began to talk at once. Maxie wished her brother-in-law hadn't asked the question. Now she was trapped. And Joe had moved his hand to her upper thigh. The way he massaged her leg drove her mad.

She had to get out of there.

"To make an interminable story long . . ."

Everybody laughed. Joe's hand inched higher. He

was dangerously close to discovering how hot and bothered he made her.

"Claude looked at me, and I knew exactly what he was thinking. As we all piled out, he yelled across the room to me, 'Hey, Maxie. You want to neck?' 'What time?' I yelled. We both lost our jobs on the spot."

"It was a hot spot, indeed," Joseph said. But before he could move his hand any higher, Maxie jumped up from the table as if the political-correctness police were chasing her.

"End of story," she said.

"Hey, aren't you staying for strawberry short-cake?" Crash said. "I made it."

"Sorry. I've got work to do. I'm on a job that I'm dying to finish."

"I'll walk you to your car." Joseph gripped her arm, knowing full well she wouldn't make a fuss in front of B. J. and Crash.

Maxie waited until they were in the front yard before she jerked out of his grip. Bending over, she snatched up two daffodils, but she was so mad she didn't even sniff them.

"What was that all about in there?" Holding the daffodils in a death grip, she shoved her hair away from her hot face. "We had an agreement."

"I was breaking the rules."

"Don't do it again."

"Why? Because you didn't like it, or because you liked it too much?"

"I'm not going to stand in my own sister's front yard and be interrogated by a lawyer."

She reached for the door handle, but Joe was quicker. Pinned between her little Beetle and his hot body, she had nowhere to turn.

"Tell me, Maxie. Is that job you're so anxious to finish, mine?"

"Yes."

The way he studied her, you'd have thought she was on trial for beheading daffodils, or worse. She lifted her chin, daring him to comment. He was silent, watching her. If there was one thing Maxie couldn't stand, it was pregnant silence, silence fraught with all sorts of unspoken sentiments and unresolved feelings.

"Decorating is my business," she said, still defiant. "It's what I do for a living. If I don't finish jobs on time, I don't pay the rent. It's that simple."

"Maxie . . . Maxie." Joe's voice was soft and chiding, as if she were a recalcitrant child.

He gently pried her fist open.

"You're crushing the daffodils."

He straightened the stems, then placed the flowers in her open palm, tenderly, in the way of a man who loves a woman.

Mesmerized, Maxie could do nothing but stand in the dark in her sister's front yard and wish for things to be different. Joe closed her fingers over the daffodils, then leaned over and kissed her on the cheek.

" 'Night, Maxie."

At his car he turned and smiled. "See you in my dreams," he said, then drove off into the night.

She stood in the yard watching until the taillights disappeared around the bend. Lifting the daffodils to her face, she inhaled. The scent of spring. The season of promise.

"See you in mine, Joe," she whispered.

FIFTEEN

Magic Maxie's was chaos. Leopard velour curtains were draped over the sofa, a matching bedspread took up most of the space on the worktable, and an assortment of carved statues stood at attention around the room. Claude surveyed his surroundings with pursed lips, then stalked to the sink and jerked up the watering pot.

"I watered those flowers yesterday," Maxie said.

Claude didn't even glance her way but kept on pouring water into the pots.

"I always water the flowers when I'm distressed. If they die, I'll buy some more."

"Don't tell me Mrs. Prescott wants everything done in burnt orange."

"It's not Mrs. Prescott I'm distressed about. It's you."

"All right. I admit I never should have taken on the Beauregard job. I wanted it done so fast, I was forced into buying retail instead of having things custom made. It was a foolhardy thing to do."

"You can be foolhardy till the cows come home, and I won't blink an eye. What's bothering me is this."

Claude jerked up one of the statues. Made of ebony, it was an African fertility God at full mast.

"What do you think Joseph Beauregard is going to do when he sees this perched beside his bed?"

"Maybe it will inspire him. Lord knows, he's going to need inspiration of that kind if he continues to squire around half the eligible women in Tupelo."

Claude cocked his head to one side and studied the statue.

"Well, honey, if that won't inspire him, I don't know what will. It's fixing to inspire me, if you don't take it out of here."

"I'll have everything loaded up within an hour, Claude."

"Mrs. Prescott is not expecting me till eleven. I'll help." He started packing boxes. "Are you finishing today?"

"Yes. And if my luck holds, I'll be out of there by midafternoon."

"Before Joseph Beauregard gets home?"

"I'm hoping."

"You'd better do some praying, too, Maxie. I wouldn't want to be within a city block of his house when he sees all this."

❦──────────────❦

The intercom on Joseph's desk buzzed.

"It's a message from Magic Maxie's," Jenny said.

"Read it."

" 'Project complete. I left the key on the bedside table.' "

"Did she say when to meet her there?"

"No, that was it."

"Nothing about the bill?"

"Nothing. . . . Will that be all, sir?"

Joseph glanced at his watch. Three-thirty. Maxie hadn't wasted any time finishing with him. That was all right with Joseph.

Redecoration wasn't what he'd had in mind when he'd hired her, but something far more meaningful, infinitely more exciting. The project was a symbol of the future, their future, together.

He could no more predict the future than when he was engaged to Susan, but it didn't matter anymore. He'd become addicted to surprise, and to the woman who provided it.

"Reschedule my afternoon appointments, Jenny."

The house was quiet when Joseph let himself in. It was Hazel's day off. Was Maxie upstairs waiting for him? Wild hope. Foolish fantasy.

Nonetheless, he took the stairs two at a time. There was magic between them. He knew she felt it. He could hear it in her voice over the phone, he could see it in her eyes every time they met, he could read it in her body language.

The door to his bedroom was closed. Joseph stood outside in the hallway, his imagination taking flight. He pictured the king-size bed, rid of its functional green cotton comforter and replaced with something lush and inviting, something that would be a perfect backdrop for the lush and inviting body of Maxie Corban.

Music filtered through the door. A jazzy tune. He listened, his heart pumping double time. Was she in there dancing? Wearing a gold bustier? Her ripe breasts begging to be touched?

He pushed open the door.

"Maxie?" The blinds were drawn, the lights off. Joseph stepped inside. "Maxie?"

There was no sign of her except the music and the lingering fragrance of her perfume, an intoxicating blend of the sweet, the spicy, and the exotic.

Joseph flipped on the lights . . . and froze. For an insane moment he thought he might be in the wrong house, or even on the wrong planet. What had once been a conservative bachelor's bedroom was now a lothario's lair. Fertility gods in full flower leered at him from every corner. Every lamp in the room sported a red-fringed shade. His bed looked like a jungle animal set to pounce, and a string of colored Christmas lights blinked at him from the headboard.

Lest he miss any small detail, mirrors on the ceiling reflected every inch of tawdry splendor.

A curtain of amber beads hung from where his bathroom door used to be.

Joseph stalked across the room and parted the curtain. Thunderstruck, he took note of what Maxie had done.

Mirrored shelves occupied one entire wall, and lined up with the precision of soldiers on review was an array of sex toys that would make Larry Flynt blush: whips and chains, handcuffs and dog collars, fishnet briefs and black lace garters, things that whirred and buzzed and pulsed, all with motors running.

Joseph went into his bedroom and snatched his key from the bedside table. A note from Maxie was attached:

"I thought you might like something in keeping with your new lifestyle. You have my personal guarantee that the room will do the trick. Enjoy!"

"That's exactly what I plan to do, Maxie."

Attached to the note was a bill on Magic Maxie's letterhead, "No Charge" written in bold red letters.

He wadded the note and bill and crammed them into his pocket. As he stalked toward the door he remembered the name of the music wafting around his bedroom: it was "Hard Hearted Hannah," Maxie's strip music.

Claude was sitting on the sofa with his feet propped up, enjoying a cup of tea when he heard the bells over the shop door. They didn't just tinkle, they clanged.

"Good grief," he said.

He jerked his feet off the table as none other than Joseph Patrick Beauregard stormed in.

"Where's Maxie?"

"Where are your manners? Whatever happened to, 'Hello, Claude. How are you today?'"

"Wild animals don't have manners. Where's Maxie?"

"She's not here."

"I can see that. I want to know where she is."

"I suppose you've checked her house?"

"She's not there. Where is she?"

"Why should I tell you? You look like a raging bull."

"I'll give you one good reason, and I'm only going to say this once: Maxie left a bill, and I intend to give her everything she has coming."

Every time Maxie went through what she called her shrinking violet stage, she took refuge in The Pottery Shed. Located ten miles from Tupelo, it was managed by Kelly Rumhouser, a late-blooming artist who had discovered her talent after being ditched by a trucker from Alabama who had fallen in love with long distances . . . and a little waitress at Denny's Truck Stop in Mobile.

A couple of years back Maxie had taken a six-week course in pottery making, and for a small monthly fee she could continue to use the studio at her leisure to work on whatever project suited her fancy.

Cheerful chaos was the best way to describe Kelly's

place. Kelly was always up to her elbows in children, pets, and clay. Her three preschoolers and their two dogs had the run of the place. They raced among the pots and platters and vases without breaking a thing.

The Blanchard sisters, both retired schoolteachers, sat at two wheels in the back of the studio arguing whether they should exhibit at the next Gum Tree Arts Festival. Eula said they weren't ready, and Tula said they'd be dead before Eula could make up her mind to take the brave step of exhibiting.

Maxie welcomed the chaos. She took a lump of clay from the freezer and plopped it on the wheel.

"I'm never going to have another relationship," she said as she pounded a lump of wet clay into submission. Kelly, a model of serenity in the midst of bedlam, merely murmured an assent as she turned a lump of clay into a delicate ballerina.

Eula and Tula perked up. They weren't one bit shy about shameless eavesdropping.

"Relationships are messy," Maxie said. She guided her clay crookedly, and her wheel began to wobble. Smashing the pieces flat, she started over.

"From now on I'm going to be a shrinking violet," she said. "I'm going to stay at home with a good book. I'm going to learn to cook gourmet food. I might even get a cat."

"Every old maid I know has a cat," Kelly said.

Maxie's wheel stopped. "What did you say?"

"You said you were going to get a cat. I said, 'Every old maid has one.' "

"That's right," Eula chimed in. "Mine's a handsome Persian, but Tula prefers Siamese."

"I'm not sure I'm planning anything that drastic."

"You said you were going to be a wallflower." Kelly dipped her hands into a nearby pail of water, then began shaping and molding. "Joyce next door has a calico cat with six kittens. She'd probably let you have one. I can call her and find out."

"We got ours in Memphis," Tula said. "Finest stock in the South. I can give you the name of the breeder."

"Cat pillows are on sale at Wal-Mart," Eula added. "I saw them yesterday when I went for Mr. Prince's catnip."

Maxie had a sudden vision of herself six years from now, sitting in a rocking chair with a lap robe over her knees and a cat in her lap, watching a phone that never rang.

"I'm not sure I'm ready for a cat just yet." She bent over her wheel and tried to wipe everything from her mind except the way the clay felt under her hands, soft and wet and malleable. She would make a teapot, then fire it and use one of the bright red glazes. Tomorrow after she'd decorated for baby Joe's party, she would drive out to her grandparents' farm and pick daffodils. Though both grandparents had been dead for years now, she and B. J. used the farm as a retreat. Going there was like stepping back in time. Daffodils covered the hillsides, multiplying each year so that every time Maxie went there she was surprised by a new patch of bright yellow blossoms.

She would lie in the pasture among the yellow flowers and look up at the sky and think of a million things, all totally unrelated to a certain man with a seductive voice and a way of looking at her that turned her world upside down.

When the door swung open, she never even looked up.

"Can I help you, sir?" Kelly said.

"No, thank you. I see exactly what I want."

Maxie jerked upright and stared straight at Joseph Patrick Beauregard. One look at his face told her that he'd seen his house. If she were Dorothy, she would close her eyes, click her heels, and wish herself back to Kansas, but she was not in a *Wizard of Oz* fantasy: She was in Tupelo, Mississippi, with a man bent on revenge, and it was time to face the music.

Joseph plowed toward her like a runaway steam engine. Maxie stiffened her spine, lifted her chin, and stood her ground.

"As you can see, I'm very busy." Joseph didn't say a word, he just kept coming. Maxie's wheel never stopped turning, but her fingers sank into the sides of her clay pot. "If I were you, I wouldn't come any closer. You're liable to get your suit dirty."

"Before this is over, lots of things are liable to get dirty."

He was beside her now, as forbidding as the Rockies with a winter storm brewing. This was a side of Joseph she'd never seen.

Maxie wet her lips with the end of her tongue. "Before what is over?"

"This."

In one swift movement he plucked her from her place behind the pottery wheel. Bits of wet clay flew in every direction. With no more effort than it would take to lift a small child, Joseph tossed her over his shoulder. Her breath whooshed out.

"What do you think you're doing?"

"Relax, Maxie. I know exactly what I'm doing."

"Put me down this instant, you blackguard." She'd never been forced to talk upside down before, and she found herself addressing his coattails. She hammered her fists on his back for emphasis, but he kept right on walking. "Joseph Patrick Beauregard, if you don't stop, there's going to be hell to pay."

"There's going to be hell to pay, all right."

With that declaration, he marched toward the front door. Kelly and the sisters looked on, stunned.

"Don't worry, ladies," Joseph said. "Maxie and I often play games together."

Kelly recovered enough to find her voice. "Do you, Maxie?"

"No. Call nine one one."

"She's such a kidder." Joseph patted her bottom. "We're practically family."

"This is kidnapping," Maxie said, pounding her fists on his back once more. She might as well have been a gnat swatting at an elephant. "I'm going to scream bloody murder if you don't put me down this instant."

"Such a bad example to set for our nephew. Have you no shame?"

Kelly looked uncertain. Holding Maxie fast with one arm, Joseph flipped a business card on her desk.

"I don't mean to alarm you. If you like, I'll wait here while you call this number. My secretaries can answer any questions you might have."

Kelly glanced from the card in her hand to the man in her shop. Romantic from the top of her head to the tip of her toes, she loved nothing more than a good drama. Most of the time she only got it from television, but today it was happening right in her shop.

"That won't be necessary," she said.

Maxie tried to glare daggers at her, but being upside down she could only glare at the back of Joe's pants. She waited until she was outside to turn loose her full fury.

"How dare you treat me like this, and in a public place. The sisters are horrible gossips. By now I'll bet half the town knows what you've done to me."

"Maxie, they don't have a clue."

His Lincoln waited at the curb. Joseph jerked open the door and stuffed her inside.

"Don't even think about trying to get out," he said, his face so close to hers that she could see the beginning of a beard's shadow already forming.

She could easily have escaped while he made his way around the car, but she didn't. Scrunched deep in the leather seats on her side of the car, she watched the man who had taken her captive. What form of insanity caused her to acquiesce? What was she doing sitting in Joseph's car when she could be in her own, racing to the safety of her own home?

He drove in tight-jawed silence while Maxie pretended an interest in the landscape. Finally she could no longer stand the suspense.

"I suppose you've seen your house." He didn't say a word, just stared straight ahead. What did his silence mean? Oblivious of the wet clay on her hands, Maxie wrapped her arms around herself to keep from shivering. "All right. So I got a little carried away. But *you* were the one who told me to do it exactly as I wanted to."

Still, nothing from Joe. The long shadows of evening closed in around the car. It didn't take a genius to figure out where they were going. The streets to Joseph's house were all too familiar.

Soon his Tudor mansion loomed before them. Maxie knew only too well what waited inside, a monster of her own creation, a playground for Tupelo's newest playboy.

But she also knew Joseph. She hoped. It was time to gamble.

"I'm not going inside," she said.

"Go in under your own power, or under mine. Take your choice."

This time of evening most of his neighbors were sitting down to dinner at their antique tables in their fancy dining rooms under the glare of Grandmother's oil portrait and her eight-light chandelier. And all in front of wide French windows that provided a sweeping view of the neighborhood, including the Tudor mansion so prominently displayed on top of a small rise.

Joseph Patrick Beauregard might be willing to use caveman tactics in front of people he didn't know in a small art studio on the wrong side of town, but he wouldn't dare pull such a stunt in his own ritzy neighborhood in front of his own snooty neighbors. Or would he?

Maxie glared at him. "You wouldn't dare."

"Are you challenging me, Maxie?" His voice was soft and deadly.

She lifted her chin. "Yes. If you want me inside your house, you're going to have to make a spectacle in front of your own friends and neighbors."

For a fleeting moment, she thought she had won. Then Joe bailed out of the car and slammed his door. She shivered as he stalked her, but she didn't budge. In this battle of wills she might not win, but she was determined to go down fighting.

SIXTEEN

Maxie didn't resist as Joseph scooped her out of the car. For a moment he thought of tossing her over his shoulder again, the neighbors be hanged. But his habits of conservatism were deeply ingrained, and deep inside was an element of caution that would not be denied. Instead, he carried her over the threshold the way a man might carry a bride. Let the neighbors chew on that.

"I can't believe you're doing this," Maxie said.

He glanced down at the bundle in his arms, red lips as enticing as ripe plums, soft skin washed with gold from the lights that automatically came on outside his house at dusk, body unbelievably lush in his arms. As furious as he was at her betrayal, as determined as he was to make her pay, he had to fight to control his passion.

"Believe it, Maxie."

"I thought you cared about public opinion."

"It won't work," he said.

"What won't work?"

"Trying to sidetrack me." Joseph strode through his front door then kicked it shut behind him. "Now there's no one to see us."

He felt the shiver that ran through her. Was it fear? Anger? Passion?

"You've got me where you want me. Put me down."

That would be the smart thing to do: set her on her own two feet so he wouldn't be tempted to turn loose the beast that raged in him. Instead he pulled her closer, holding her so tightly, she sucked in her breath. It was a dangerous thing to do, but then, so was kidnapping.

"I'll put you down when I'm ready." Her eyes widened. "Haven't you caught on, Maxie? Tonight I'm calling all the shots."

"What game are you playing?"

"This is no game. This is real."

He strode toward the stairs with Maxie in his arms, resolute. In his bedroom the music was playing, just as he'd left it, a bawdy, raucous song that set the mood for this evening where anything could happen.

He kicked his bedroom door open and strode to the middle of the room.

"Take a good look, Maxie."

"I've already seen it. I'm the one who did it, remember?"

"How could I forget."

Keeping a tight grip on her, he went to his bed and

held her suspended over the wild jungle animal that passed for a coverlet.

"What are you doing?" she said.

"Testing my new lair." He lowered her a few inches. "Feel the bedcovers, Maxie. . . . Go on . . . put your hand on them."

Slowly, reluctantly, she spread her fingers and swept them over the velour coverlet.

"What does it feel like, Maxie?"

"A wild animal."

"Very good. And what do wild animals do to bad little girls? . . . Come on. Don't you remember your fairy tales?"

"This is not a fairy tale. This is real, and you're being a beast."

"Right again, Maxie. A beast you created." He dipped her until her bottom was touching the mattress. "You still haven't told me what wild animals do to bad little girls."

Her chin went up. "They eat them."

"That's exactly right . . . and I'm very hungry."

He let that bit of information sink in, watching her closely, judging her reaction by the widening of her eyes, the flaring of her nostrils, the flush of her skin. His passion stirred. What had he expected? Maxie always ignited him.

Still, he wasn't about to be sidetracked. His aim was revenge, not release.

But Maxie was a worthy opponent. Clenching her jaw, she closed her fist around a wad of velour.

"You're forgetting one thing, Joseph Beauregard.

I'm no Little Red Riding Hood. If you think I'll lie on this bed for you to paw over, you'd better think again."

He laughed without mirth. "I never believed you would be an easy prey. You've just proved me right."

He lowered her all the way to the mattress and pinned her to the bed, arms stretched over her head, legs weighted down with his knee.

She wet her lips with the tip of her tongue. "Look, I admit I might have gone too far, but I can put it back to its original condition. No charge, of course."

"What you've done is perfectly suitable for my purposes."

He'd thought she might come up scratching and clawing. Instead she lay perfectly still, matching him stare for stare.

"You left some nice toys in the bathroom," he said. She defied him with stillness. "Can you be trusted to stay here while I fetch them? . . . I thought not."

He reached into the bedside table and pulled out the handcuffs. "You know what these are for, don't you?"

A trickle of sweat rolled down the side of her cheek.

"You know, Joseph, there was a moment when I almost changed my mind about doing this bedroom."

Blood roared in his ears so loudly, he wondered that he could hear. What if she really did feel something for him, something besides contempt? What if he still had one slim chance with her, only one, and he was blowing it tonight?

"I almost backed out. . . ." She bathed her bottom lip with the tip of her tongue. Joseph bit back a groan. "I almost changed my mind, right after we started that telephone relationship."

The words hung in the air between them. He remembered those late-night calls, the passion that bloomed swiftly, surely, the hot words that teased, incited. Desire exploded through him, and he bit back another groan.

They stared at each other, riveted, uncertain. Her chin came up.

"I'm glad I didn't," she said.

The last vestige of hope shattered inside him, and Joseph hardened his heart. He snapped on the cuffs and chained her to the bedpost.

"So am I," he said. With slow deliberation he unbuttoned her blouse.

"What are you doing?"

He'd have to hand it to her. Maxie was either totally unmoved by his actions or she was a great actress.

"I'm taking what you promised." He pushed the material aside and ran his fingers lightly across the tops of her breasts. She shivered. At last, a reaction.

"I never promised you anything. We had an agreement: All sex would be confined to the telephone, and then only as long as we both wanted it."

"This is not about telephone sex."

She waited, watching him. Long ago he'd learned that often the best tactic with an opponent was to let him squirm.

He waited, watching her. But she didn't squirm. In

fact, if the soft flush that came over her skin was any indication, she was as excited as he was.

It was too bad, and too late. Once Joe committed himself to a course of action, there was no turning back.

She was the first to break the silence. "All right, then. I apologize. Is that what you want? I'm sorry I ever turned your nice conservative bedroom suite into a jungle playground, and I'll have it put back in two days."

"Maxie . . . Maxie . . ."

"What? What is it you want from me? A pound of flesh?"

"Not a bad idea."

He unsnapped the front of her bra. Her breasts were lush and ripe, nipples as hard as diamonds. He rubbed his palm over those hard, inviting peaks, testing her, testing himself. But there were limits to what a man could endure without caving in.

He stood up, pulled her note out of his pocket, and let it flutter to the bed.

"This is what I want, Maxie." He held it in front of her face so she could read it. "You gave your personal guarantee, and I've brought you here to collect."

A flush the color of roses crept across her skin. Her eyes were so bright, he didn't dare return her stare.

Leaving her handcuffed to the bed, he went into the bathroom and splashed water on his face. Then he leaned over the sink and reined in his galloping hunger.

What was she doing out there on his bed? What

was she thinking? He straightened up, listening, but there were no sounds from his bedroom except the music.

He grabbed a handful of toys from the mirrored shelves. As he turned to go back into the bedroom he glimpsed himself in the mirror. With his disheveled hair and burning eyes he looked every inch the beast she'd called him. Was this what happened when a man fell in love only to have all his dreams shattered? Had he turned into some sort of wild animal who could think of nothing but his own monstrous passion?

He cracked the whip against his thigh so hard, he felt the sting of leather through his trousers. Through an opening in the beaded curtain he could see Maxie on his bed, every enticing inch of her reflected in the mirrors on his ceiling.

When he'd brought her to his house earlier in the evening he'd had some half-cocked idea about exacting revenge. About teaching her a lesson.

The person who had learned the lesson was himself. He couldn't go back in there and take her like a beast. She was wild and free, as uninhibited as any woman he'd ever met. She didn't give a whit for public opinion, and never passed up an opportunity to defy convention, to shock her onlookers. Hauling her out of the art studio caveman-style was no humiliation for her. Nor had he intended it to be. He was saving all that for the privacy of his bedroom. And she lay chained to his bed, waiting.

But suddenly he had no heart for his task, no taste for revenge. The game was over. All bets were off.

For a brief shining time, he and Maxie had been lovers. But only on the telephone. Only in his dreams.

The dream had ended the moment he'd stepped into his bedroom suite. Instead of designing a cozy retreat for two people in love, she'd designed a lair for a lone wolf. Maxie not only didn't share his dream, but she disdained the dreamer.

He took one last glimpse through the curtain, and the ache of love lost almost brought him to his knees. Gone was the dream of Maxie waking beside him with the early-morning sun in her hair. Gone was the dream of her wrapped in his arms beside a winter fire. Gone was the dream of her bending over the tub, laughing as she took her first step into the hot soapy water, teasing him with a glance over her shoulder. "Now that the children are asleep, we can play," she would say.

He shoved aside the beads and strode to the bed, the whip still curled in his fist.

"I might have known you'd choose that first," she said.

"Why?"

"Because you like to be in control."

She had no idea how close she was to the truth, and how close he'd come to losing the very thing he prided himself on.

"Maxie, no one will ever control you. Do you know why?"

"You tell me."

"I chained your body to the bed, but I couldn't chain your mind." He knelt beside her and brushed her hair back from her damp forehead, tenderly, in the way of a man who has loved a woman deeply and truly, in the way of a lover saying good-bye. "No one will ever be able to chain your mind, Maxie."

Taking the keys from his pocket, he unsnapped the handcuffs. He turned quickly, before he could see her face, before he could change his mind, and picked up the telephone.

"What are you doing?"

"I'm calling a cab for you."

She reached around him and punched the disconnect button. It was his turn to be surprised. He looked over his shoulder at her.

"I'll call my own cab." She ran her hands up the back of his neck and into his hair. He felt the shock waves all the way to his toes.

She hopped off the bed and planted herself in front of him, hands on her hips, blouse gaping open, chin tipped back, hips thrust forward.

"Maxie . . . what are you doing?"

"I gave my personal guarantee, and Magic Maxie always delivers what she promises."

She bent over the bed and picked up the whip.

SEVENTEEN

The handle of the whip was leather, and still warm where Joseph had gripped it. She slid her hands along the heated leather, taking courage, buying time.

What in the world was she doing? Why wasn't she taking the fastest exit? Joseph was letting her off easy.

He sat on the edge of the bed, not speaking, not moving, but watching her with an expression as distant and inscrutable as the moon. From the time Maxie could walk and talk, she'd depended on her instincts. People called her madcap and spontaneous and sometimes things not so kind, but what they didn't know was that she always did what her instincts dictated. She didn't try to analyze, didn't sit down and think things through, didn't weigh the pros and cons, didn't make long lists like her sister and then spend days revising them. Right or wrong, good or bad, Maxie did exactly what her instincts told her.

Sometimes she regretted her actions, as she did

with Joseph's bedroom. Just as often she was thrilled, as she had been when she'd left Atlanta and set up her own firm. A rash action that appeared wrongheaded at the time had led to the establishment of Magic Maxie's.

She didn't know what today's rash action would lead to. All she knew was that she had to follow her instincts. And they all led straight to Joseph.

She popped the whip lightly along the side of her hip. "Why, Joseph?"

"Just leave, Maxie."

"No. Not without answers."

"I don't even know the questions, let alone the answers."

The muted whisper of leather against flesh competed with the sound of music, filling the silence that stretched between them. Mirrored tiles in the ceiling caught them in poses of indecision, frozen mere inches apart from each other, paralyzed by emotions too raw, too wild, too new.

From somewhere deep in the house a grandfather clock struck the hour, and outside a sliver of a moon floated above the oak tree and hung there, suspended on branches green with spring leaves.

Maxie put one foot on the path, then the other. Joseph sucked in a sharp breath. Blindly, following instinct, Maxie moved irrevocably toward the bed, toward the unknown.

On many nights such as this they'd played games, they'd teased and taunted each other into a sexual frenzy, they'd found release via the telephone. But every time they were together, an invisible wall appeared between them. They moved toward the brink, and pulled back.

"Maxie." Joseph's voice held a warning.

"Don't you dare say it. Don't you dare tell me to stop."

"No more games."

"You're right." Maxie threw the whip and it landed with a loud clunk on the floor. "This is not a game."

She advanced until she was standing directly in front of him, knees touching. Body heat radiated from him, warming her, giving her courage.

"Look at me." Slowly she unfastened the last of her buttons. Bending close, she pulled his face to her breast.

"For you," she whispered.

He caught her around the waist and held her back. "Don't tempt me, Maxie."

"Why not?"

"Don't ask."

She covered his hands and wove her fingers between his. "All right, then. No questions, no answers, no more talk." Kneeling in front of him, she unzipped his pants. "Just sex."

"Maxie . . . my God."

He pulsed against her hand, and she held him tenderly, in the way of a woman who loves a man. The knowledge flashed through her like a comet. She loved this man. She'd loved him from the first moment she saw him, months earlier, standing in the midst of Tupelo's elite with his fiancée at his side. Mr. Perfect, she'd called him. And he was. No matter his flaws, no matter hers.

And now it was too late, too late for tender words, too late for proclamations, too late for commitment, too late for anything except good-bye. Maxie was determined to make it a good-bye worth remembering.

Still on her knees, she bent her face toward the dark mysteries she'd uncovered, bent her face toward the sweet, secret warmth and touched him tenderly with her tongue. The shiver started in his legs and stretched upward, to his chest, his arms, his hands, his face, even his hair. Maxie felt this power she had over him and smiled, not with wicked glee, not with triumph, but with a sadness that came from knowing she'd made a remarkable discovery too late, far too late.

"This is madness, Maxie." Joseph caught her face between his palms and tipped it upward. "Stop now, before it's too late."

For an instant he circled his thumbs on her cheeks, then he circled her waist, pulled her upright and held her at arm's length.

"It's already too late, Joseph. Don't you know that?"

A muscle in the side of his jaw ticked. She could almost see the workings of his mind, could imagine him turning over all the possibilities of her statement. He was too smart not to know what she was talking about.

It was too late for them. They had nothing left to lose.

"Button your blouse, Maxie."

"You unbuttoned it. If you want it fastened, you're going to have to do it yourself."

He towered over her, his face a thundercloud. There was no gentleness in his movement as he reached for her blouse.

"First the bra," she said.

"What?"

"You also undid my bra. You have to fasten it back first."

"Be careful what you ask, Maxie."

"I'm never cautious. Don't you know that by now? Good, bad, or indifferent, I always do and say whatever occurs to me at the moment."

She was talking to fill up time, talking to cover up her own nervousness. Now that she had committed herself to this course of action, she was having second thoughts.

"Live for the moment," Joe said. "I've never been an advocate . . ." His eyes swept over her, lingering on her naked breasts. "But if any woman could convert me, it's you."

In a swift unexpected move that took her breath away, he bent down and laved her nipple with his tongue. She wound her hands in his hair and pulled him closer.

"Maxie . . . Maxie . . ."

His mouth covering her, his tongue hot on her skin, he devoured her. Weak-kneed she grabbed his shoulders and hung on.

He moved from one breast to the other, leaving a

trail of hot kisses across her chest. The room became a kaleidoscope of sounds and colors and textures—his dark hair against her creamy skin, his deep-throated murmurings and her soft keen of pleasure, a flash of lightning in the darkened sky followed by raindrops tapping at the window, the whisper of clothing, the bright pink of silk pooling against the carpet, the plush feel of velour as Joe lowered her to the bed.

Kneeling over her, he studied her eyes.

"Are you sure this is what you want?"

Maxie wasn't about to give him the satisfaction of thinking he'd triumphed over her, that he'd won an easy victory, or any victory at all, for that matter. Nor did she want him to think that she was asking for things she knew they would never have.

"Yes, as long as you understand that this is nothing personal."

His eyebrow quirked upward. "Nothing personal?"

She lifted her stubborn chin. "Absolutely not. You started something and for once you're going to finish it. That's all." She wet her lower lip with the tip of her tongue. "This is purely sexual. Nothing more."

Instead of answering he pressed his hips into hers. She could feel the power of him, the heat, the overwhelming passion.

"As long as you understand that," she whispered. "Agreed?"

"I've agreed to nothing, Maxie."

Using the tip of his finger, he drew a line from the center of her lips to the tiny pulse point in her throat.

Shivers raced along her spine, raised the hair on her arms and along the back of her neck. She lay perfectly still, not daring to move, hardly daring to breathe lest the spell be broken.

With maddening deliberation he drew tiny erotic circles at the base of her throat, then moved downward, into the valley between her breasts. Her skin heated up, her face flushed, and she wondered if he could feel the galloping rhythm of her heart.

"You like that, don't you, Maxie?" She decided silence was her best defense. "You don't have to answer, your body says it all."

He dragged his fingertips along the crests of her breasts, pausing to tease her nipples.

"Say it," she whispered. "Say this is nothing except sex, pure and simple."

His mouth turned up at the corners in what might have passed as a smile if she hadn't known him so well. There was no light in his eyes, no mirth in his face, no sense of joy in the quick harsh bark of laughter.

He pinched her nipple between his thumb and forefinger, exerting just enough pressure to enflame her already overheated body.

"You'd like that, wouldn't you, Maxie? You'd like to have what you want, then walk out of here with no residual feelings. No guilt, no remorse, no thought to consequences."

"Yes." She felt as if her blood were on fire. If Joe didn't do something soon, she'd scream. "Just say it . . . say this is sex, pure and simple, and be done with it."

"I would be lying. There's nothing at all pure about my motives."

He peeled her skirt down her legs, then hooked his thumb under the waistband of her panties. Gazing deep into her eyes, his thumbs pressed hot circles on her skin.

"When I mount you, Maxie, when you spread your legs and start that sensual journey that leads to sweet, slow death, it will not be simple." He stripped her panties off, his eyes glowing like hot coals. "It will not be simple at all."

He stared down at her as if he were trying to decide whether to eat her or truss her up and burn her at the stake as if she were one of Salem's witches. Then, lionlike he crouched over her and buried his face in her mound of soft dark curls. She burned, she soared, she trembled.

His name was on the tip of her tongue, but she was too full to speak, too full of burning pleasure, of vaulting freedom, of volcanic passion. She tangled her hands in his hair, weaving her fingers through the dark strands.

"You taste the way I imagined you would, like some exotic fruit," he said.

"Don't talk."

She arched toward his questing tongue, caught up in a hurricane of passion that swept her into another realm.

"This is not enough," Joe murmured. "Not enough."

He shed his clothes in swift, efficient movements,

then lifted himself over her, as magnificent as any man she'd ever seen.

"Say no," he said. "Tell me to stop."

"I can't . . . I won't."

He entered her in one swift, sure stroke, burying himself so deep that she was impaled. Pieces of her heart broke off and flew to nestle in his, and she knew that no matter what happened in the days and weeks and years to come, Joseph Patrick Beauregard would always have a part of her, the best part.

She wanted everything at once, the long, slow strokes, the hot, hard pounding. She wanted him to kiss her and suckle her at the same time. Impossible task. She wanted his mouth and hands all over her. But most of all she wanted the strong silent lover who heaved above her, carrying her on a journey that she would remember forever.

The mirrored ceiling captured the reflection of two people, arms and legs entangled, bodies parting and merging, parting and merging, locked forever in the slow, sweet dance of love.

Her hair was like flame on the jungle-animal coverlet, like fire shooting from her head, and she felt as if her entire body had ignited. *I don't want this ever to end*, she thought, but she could not say the words aloud, *would* not say them aloud.

An old adage her grandmother had taught her played through her mind: Pride goeth before a fall. Maxie knew it was true. Both she and her sister had experienced it firsthand many times. "If there is one thing I've tried to teach you," her grandmother used to say, "it's not to be too prideful, too willful. Lordy, lordy, it looks like I've failed."

B. J. had finally learned to swallow her pride, and look at the prize she won: an adoring husband and an angelic baby.

But Maxie knew she could never swallow hers. If she thought about that too hard, if she thought about the price she was paying, she might start crying.

"Don't think," she told herself. Don't think about anything except this man who filled her heart, body, and soul.

He was a silent lover. She didn't know whether that was his usual way, or whether his silence was only for this night, for this brief encounter that served as both a beginning and an end.

They tangled the covers around them, then kicked them free again, never stopping their heady journey, never pausing in the hot, headlong rush toward the stars. Tension gathered in her, twisted her inside out, built until it was an explosion that wrenched cries from both of them. Sweat-slick and sated, she clung to him, breathless. He buried his face in her hair, still silent, and when she saw his reflection on the ceiling, it looked as if he were praying.

She wanted to comfort him, to murmur words of reassurance, to whisper words of love and commitment. Her hands hovered inches above his head, suspended in the heavy silence of that exotic room where two bodies still lay joined.

With a groan Joseph stirred. He gripped her close, fiercely, then pulled away. Maxie felt bereft.

For one brief, shining moment he had been hers, all hers. Her body would carry his imprint for the rest of her life, and at night when she lay in her small empty bed in her little yellow house on Maxwell Street, she would think of this moment, of the two of them together, slick with sweat, their love juices mingled.

Joseph reached for his clothes and Maxie reached for hers. They didn't look at each other, didn't speak. What was there left to say?

She heard him in the bathroom, the sound of running water, the flushing of the toilet. Small, everyday things.

"Life goes on." Another of her grandmother's sayings. Maxie hoped it was true.

The beaded curtain rattled, parted. Joseph looked untouched by what had occurred on the bed.

"I'll take you home," he said.

Maxie nodded. She didn't know whether home meant her house or her car. She didn't care. All she knew was that she had to get through the rest of her life, one moment at a time.

EIGHTEEN

Maxie dressed in red. It was a color that always made her feel better. She made herself eat a good breakfast, made herself read the morning paper, made herself turn on the stereo so her house was filled with music. Little things. Ordinary things. Minute by minute she would get by. She would live her life one day at a time, and soon when she woke in the morning she wouldn't be overwhelmed with memories of Joe. The way he looked, the way he tasted, the way he smelled.

As she lifted her coffee cup she fancied she could still smell him on her skin, even after a long, hot shower and a thorough soaping. Her hand trembled as she set the cup down.

"Don't think about him," she told herself. "It's over."

She was glad when the phone rang. It was her sister.

"Maxie, can you come over and help me?"

"Sure. What's up?"

"I just need help, that's all. The baby had colic all night, and neither of us got any sleep. Then Joe called early this morning, and Crash had to leave."

"Joe?" Maxie had to put her hand over her heart to stop its racing. "Is everything all right?"

Maxie pictured Joe, despondent over last night, calling his brother for advice. What would he do? What would he say? Would he tell his brother everything?

"Sure," B. J. said, dashing Maxie's dreams. "It was just some business matter. Crash thought it could wait till next week, but you know Joe."

Did she ever know Joe. Better than her sister would ever imagine . . . or know.

"Maxie . . . are you still there?"

"I'm here."

"What's the matter? You sound funny."

"I think I'm getting a summer cold."

"It's not summer yet."

Trust B. J. to act like a lawyer. "Well, a spring cold, then."

"Do you have any lemon juice and honey in the house? That'll make your throat feel better."

It wasn't Maxie's throat that hurt, but she didn't tell her sister.

"Look, maybe you shouldn't come over here with a cold. I don't want baby Joe catching anything."

"What I have is not contagious."

"How do you know? Have you already seen a doctor?"

"Good grief."

There was a brief silence, and then the sisters began to laugh.

"I know, I know," B. J. said. "I sound just like Grandma. Look, come on over. Newborns hardly ever catch colds. The mother's milk gives them immunity."

Maxie felt guilty. She didn't want her sister worrying needlessly, even over something as trivial as a cold.

"B. J., I'm not coming down with anything except the blues."

"The water will be hot when you get here. We'll sit in the kitchen over a cup of tea, and you can tell me about it."

B. J.'s kitchen was a cozy mixture of the old and the new, old brick floor and shining marble countertops, potbellied stove and stainless steel sink, Italian tiles and mirrored flashing. They sat at a round oak table with carved legs and sipped bracing hot tea topped with mint fresh from the garden.

"You don't look tired," Maxie said. "You look absolutely glowing."

"The fatigue is temporary, the glow is permanent." B. J. twisted the wedding ring on her finger. "How could one woman be so lucky. A fabulous husband, a wonderful son. I'm terribly, madly in love with both of them."

"Gee, I'd never have guessed."

B. J. set her cup on the table and laced her fingers

around it. "Just listen to me, going on like somebody crazy. We're here to talk about you, not me."

"There's nothing to talk about."

"Are you sure?"

"Don't look at me that way. This is not a court of law."

"Sorry. Old habits die hard." B. J. sipped her tea. "We used to share everything."

"That was when we were young and foolish and didn't know any better."

"If that's your way of telling me to mind my own business, I can take a hint."

Contrite, Maxie covered her sister's hand. "I didn't mean that the way it sounded. You're my best friend, you know that."

"Okay. No more inquisitions." B. J. set down her tea. "Let's go to the nursery so Joe can make another conquest."

"He already has. He stole my heart the minute I laid eyes on him."

It was true. What she didn't tell her sister, though, was that she was talking about both Joes, baby and uncle.

Following B. J.'s lead, she went up the stairs to the nursery, taking one step at a time.

Crash sat in the same wing chair Maxie had sat in. Joe looked at his brother, but all he could see was the outrageous Maxie, legs crossed, teasing him, taunting him, maddening him.

He picked up a pen then slammed it back onto the desk. It bounced on the smooth surface, then rolled onto the floor.

"Whoa! There's no need to get so mad. It's only business."

Though it was business they were discussing—Joe wanted Crash to be his law partner—it was love that haunted Joseph's mind. Love in the form of a red-haired siren, who in the course of one night had landed him in both heaven and hell. He forced her from his mind.

"You always take that cavalier attitude. When are you going to grow up, Nat? You have a family to think of now."

Joseph only called his brother Nat when he was particularly disturbed.

"That's exactly what I'm thinking of." Crash leaned forward in his chair. "I'd be home with them right now if you hadn't called at some god-awful hour this morning and insisted that I come down here."

"I wouldn't have called you if it weren't important."

"Great Caesar in a goat cart. This is Saturday. Nobody in his right mind goes to the office on Saturday."

"Are you saying I'm out of my mind?"

"If the shoe fits, wear it."

Crash jumped out of his chair and prowled the room. He'd had very little sleep, and he wasn't about to be easy on his brother.

"Just because you've chosen to bury yourself in the

country and ignore your God-given talent doesn't mean I have to follow suit."

"I didn't bury myself. It's called living. Something you obviously don't know much about."

The truth stung, but Joseph wasn't about to admit it. After the previous night he was resigning from life. He was going to concentrate on what he did best, being a successful lawyer. And he was determined to convert his brother. For Crash's sake.

"My Lord, Crash, with your flair for drama you'd be the best litigator in the country. I'm offering you the chance of a lifetime."

"No. What you're offering me is prison."

"Practicing law is no prison."

"The way you do it, it is. Just look at you. Pale as a ghost. Hollow-eyed. I'll bet you were up all night working on some dry and boring brief."

He was up all night, all right, but not because of the law. Thinking of Maxie in his bed, Joseph suppressed a groan.

"You have a wife now, a child. Have you thought about the future, Nat?"

Crash looked exactly like their Granddaddy Beauregard, staring at Joseph that way, staring past all the posturing and posing, staring past all the subterfuge and lies, staring straight through to his soul. He was thoughtful for such a long time that Joseph actually felt uncomfortable. His first thought was "What a talent lost." His second was "I could never fool my brother."

"I've thought about my future, Joe. Have you?"

"Of course I have." His answer was too quick, too glib. Crash would see right through it. "I planned my life years ago. Look around you, Crash." Joseph made a sweeping gesture that encompassed his expensive furniture, the rich accessories, jade vases, handmade Oriental carpets, fine paintings. "This is my life, just as I planned. I like nice things, and I work hard so I can have them. You can too."

Crash settled back into the chair and closed his eyes. For a moment Joseph thought he had gone to sleep. Then he turned another laser stare on his brother.

"Do you ever get lonely, Joe?"

"Of course. Every bachelor has his lonely moments. But the freedom more than makes up for it."

Another glib answer, spoken too quickly.

"Do you ever long to go to sleep at night beside a woman whose mind is as exciting as her body? Do you ever wish you could wake up in the morning with that same woman and start the day making slow, sweet love just because one of you reached out and touched the other's shoulder?"

Joseph had a powerful vision of Maxie, hair like flames across his pillow. Only iron control kept him in his chair. Only a powerful will kept him from howling like a caged animal.

His laughter was hollow. "Spoken like a true bridegroom. I would expect nothing less from you than a glowing recommendation for the blind and blissful state of holy matrimony."

"Great Caesar's forked tail, when did you get to be

such a cynic?" Crash gave him another piercing assessment. "This doesn't have anything to do with Maxie, does it?"

"Susan is the woman I was engaged to."

"I know that. But you didn't change one whit when you were seeing her, not even your tired old habit of having spaghetti every Wednesday night."

"What you call tired old habits happens to be a sensible routine that worked well for me, something I seem to have forgotten in the last few days."

"You didn't answer my question."

"I don't think it merits an answer."

Suddenly Crash began to laugh.

"What's so damned funny?"

"You." He wiped the mirth from his eyes, then started into fresh gales of laughter. "Maybe there's hope for you yet, Joe."

"I was hoping I could say the same thing about you, but you insist on treating my offer of a partnership as if it were an invitation to a hanging."

Crash glanced at his watch, then stood up. "Look, Joe, I appreciate the thought, and if I wanted to grind away the rest of my life in law, I can't think of a better place to do it than here or a better person to do it with than my brother. But the fact is, I'm happy with my life and I'm secure about my future. I'll never have as much money as you, but I'm far richer. Think about that, bro."

Joseph put his hand on his brother's shoulder as they walked toward the door.

"Don't say no to my offer yet. Talk it over with

your wife. Give it some thought. Promise me that much."

"I'll do that if you'll promise me something in return."

"Anything."

"Go home, get some rest, and while you're relaxing think about why you're hell-bent on avoiding the woman you couldn't keep your hands off of at my house the other night."

If Joe hadn't been such a good lawyer, he'd have had a hard time keeping his poker face. Crash winked at him.

"Been there, done that, bro."

Though it was a warm spring night outside, Joseph had turned on the gas logs in the fireplace. The *Wall Street Journal* lay in his lap, unread, and a glass of red wine sat on the table beside him, untouched. This was a routine that usually relaxed him, but he was still unnerved by his morning discussion with his brother.

Any fool should know why he was avoiding Maxie. He was water and she was oil. They simply didn't mix. Why had he ever thought he could change? Why had he ever dreamed he could cast off his conservative nature and become a man-about-town?

Besides all that, his bedroom suite made it perfectly clear what she thought of him.

He sipped his wine, then jerked open his paper, determined to read it from front to back. He gave up on the second page.

"Dammit."

He felt like a person who had been raised by wolves, neither man nor beast. He had failed at being a bohemian, and now he was equally uncomfortable being an archconservative.

That woman was driving him crazy.

The clock struck ten, and he marched upstairs. Since he couldn't do anything else, he might as well go to bed.

The minute he stepped into his bedroom he knew he wouldn't sleep again tonight. Maxie was everywhere, in the mirrored ceiling, in the wild-animal spread, in the whip that still lay on the floor. He stretched full length across his bed, fully dressed, shoes and all.

Her fragrance still lingered on the covers. His arousal was instant.

What was she doing tonight? Was she remembering?

She had been magic, pure and simple. The minute he'd entered her he'd known he'd been lying to himself. He knew that what they shared was more than passion, more than their bodies, more than sex. It was love.

Groaning, he pressed his fingers into his aching temples. He had to get organized. He had to make plans for getting on with his life. He'd start Monday morning by going to the office early and catching up on some case work he'd let slide in the last few days. But there was something else he had to do.

Somewhere in Tupelo was a man who had drunk beer from Maxie's other gold shoe, a man who at this very moment possessed the shoe as if it were some prize in a gladiator's tournament.

Joe was going to get that shoe back.

NINETEEN

His search led him to a man called Bruiser McCain, who had his own garage and wrecker service. He stood six feet, five inches, and weighed enough to crush small cars with his bare hands. Joseph knew immediately that he had the wrong man, but how did you tell a man named Bruiser that you were wasting his time? And on a Sunday-afternoon, at that?

Bruiser squinted at Joseph from underneath the visor of a baseball cap that proclaimed "This is not roadkill, it's my face."

"What can I do for you, buster?"

Joseph had never been called buster, not even when he was in third grade, but he wasn't about to make a point of his name with this man.

"I was taking a Sunday-afternoon drive and thought I heard a knocking under my hood."

"You either did or you didn't. Which is it?"

"I definitely did."

Bruiser rubbed his beard stubble and gazed into the distance. "It being Sunday and all, and me just being here to sorta straighten things up, it'll cost you."

"How much?"

"That depends."

Joe wasn't about to get into a long recital of why Bruiser was going to charge him an outrageous amount. He merely nodded, then pulled his Lincoln into the garage and watched while the top half of Bruiser disappeared under the hood.

"Don't see nothing out of the way under here," he said. " 'Course that don't always mean nothing." His head emerged briefly. "What you doin' in these parts, anyhow, a city feller like you, all slicked up?"

"I'm looking for a man who might know something about a gold shoe."

"You planning on wearin' it or what?"

"No. I'm planning to buy it."

"It must be mighty important to you, this here gold shoe."

"You could say that."

Bruiser disappeared under the hood once more, made clicking noises with his tongue, then came out once more.

"Could be I know somethin' about that shoe."

"I would be most appreciative for any information you could give me."

"How appreciative?"

Joseph held out a folded twenty. Bruiser scratched his belly, his beard, his head, then vanished under the hood.

"Tell you what," he said, his voice muffled by the cavernous interior of the Lincoln. "I'm gonna fix that knock for free." He reached into his tool belt and pulled out a hammer. A couple of taps, and he came out smiling. "I don't 'spect you'll have any more trouble out of that baby."

"Thank you."

"Don't thank me yet, I ain't through with you." Bruiser slung a beefy arm around Joe's shoulder, leaving a streak of grease on his sleeve. "I'm fixin' to give you 'bout a hunnerd dollars' worth of advice. Fair enough?"

"Fair enough." Joe pulled out a hundred-dollar bill, and Bruiser grabbed it in his big paw.

"On up the road apiece you're gonna find a man with that gold shoe you're so all-fired hot to get your hands on. Don't let on there's anything personal about the shoe, don't even talk about it, just pull out a couple more of these babies, and tell him old Bruiser said you was to buy that shoe."

Joseph guessed that word had spread to Pontotoc that he was interested in the shoe. Clearly, as the old adage said, they had seen him coming. Still, three hundred dollars was a small price to pay for winning back the trophy.

As he pulled into the driveway of the small red brick house half a mile from Bruiser's garage, he recognized the man coming out the door, the shoe already in his hand.

"That will be the last time you'll ever touch anything that belongs to Maxie," Joseph said. Then he went to claim what was rightly his.

Maxie sat in the middle of her bed with three romance novels, a six-pack of chocolate bars with almonds, a bowl of buttered popcorn, and a chocolate milkshake. Ever since that fateful night at Joseph's she had been consoling herself with junk food. If it weren't for the forty-five minutes a day she spent on her exercise bike, she'd be as big as her house.

Wallowing in self-pity, that's what she was doing. She was going to indulge herself another two weeks, and then she was going to snap out of it, as her grandmother always used to say.

She broke a chocolate bar in half, took a big bite, and turned to chapter twenty of *From a Distance*—Brett, doomed to love his brother's wife, trying to find release in the arms of another woman.

She reached for her box of tissues—Maxie, doomed to love Joseph, trying to find relief in paperback romance and chocolate.

The telephone interrupted her binge.

"Hello." Her voice was muffled by the tissue.

"Maxie?"

Books, tissue, and chocolate bars flew every which way as Maxie leaped from the bed. She wasn't about to be flat on her back when she talked to this man. It was far too dangerous.

She cleared her throat, then stuffed the tissue into the pocket of her robe. "Yes, Joseph. It's me."

Why was he calling? Why?

"How are you, Maxie?"

"Just fine." That made her sound like some little old lady recovering from the flu. "Great! I'm absolutely great."

"What are you doing this evening?"

Her bed looked as if it had been taken over by a flock of spinsters.

"Clearing up some paperwork for the business," she lied. "Tax season, you know."

"What are you wearing?"

His voice was deep, seductive. Time spun backward, and she was lying in her bed, phone cradled against her ear, listening to the secret, erotic instructions of Joseph Patrick Beauregard.

She felt herself go hot all over, then cold. For a crazy moment she thought her legs would buckle. She sank onto the edge of her bed, knuckles white as she gripped the phone.

"I won't be sucked back into that game."

"That was certainly not my intent. Let me rephrase the question: Are you still dressed?"

Her pink terry cloth robe hung unbelted, and her purple baby doll pajamas had a tear in the hem where she'd caught it on the corner of a kitchen cabinet while she was making her chocolate milkshake.

"Yes. I'm dressed." She shucked her robe and the bottoms of her baby dolls, even as she spoke.

"Good . . ."

What did he mean? Good? Her purple baby doll top billowed around her like the petals of a flower as she studied her chipped toenail polish and pondered his motives.

"Maxie? Are you still there?"

"Yes."

"Can I come over?"

In one fell swoop she raked the books off the sheets and shoved them under the bed. Then she tossed the chocolate into the popcorn bowl and shoved it next to the books. Three minutes to dress, one to race to the kitchen and dump her milkshake, two to make the bed. How long was the drive from his house to hers? She was so agitated, she'd forgotten.

"Why?" she asked, recovering her sanity.

"I have something you want."

She had to bite her lower lip to keep from groaning. Did he ever have something she wanted. Her fingers closed over the pillow, and she hugged it to her chest. She pictured the two of them tangled in her small bed, Joe's feet hanging over the end, her hands gripping the iron railings, sweat dripping off his brow and onto hers, the little bed rocking and swaying.

But just how many good-byes could she stand?

"You can come, but only for a few minutes."

"That's time enough."

Paralyzed, Maxie stared at the dead receiver. Time enough for what?

TWENTY

Her skirt was black and short, her sweater red and fuzzy, her earrings purple and dangly. She was barefoot, her hair in a ponytail tied with a purple ribbon. There was something that looked like gold dust caught up in her red toenail polish.

Joseph couldn't take his eyes off Maxie's feet. They were tiny and perfectly shaped, with delicate blue veins crisscrossing a very high instep. He wanted to kneel and kiss each blue vein. Then he wanted to suckle her toes.

"That was quick," she said, referring of course to his hell-bent-for-leather rush across town.

"Do you always work at home barefoot?"

She wiggled her toes, and he realized he was still standing in her doorway staring at her feet. Quickly he moved his gaze up to her face. Mistake. Her lips were rounded in a perfect O of surprise. He pictured them pressed against a telephone receiver, and worse, circled around him.

"Sometimes." She made a sweeping gesture around her room. "Won't you sit down? I made hot tea."

She escaped to the kitchen. Was it because she couldn't bear to look at him for the same reasons he couldn't bear to look at her, or was it because she despised him?

Joseph chose the sofa, hoping she would, too, hoping she would sit close enough for him to smell her fragrance, to feel her leg brushing against his. For a man bent on burying himself in his work, he was acting irrationally.

"Fool. Just give her the shoe and leave," he muttered.

"Did you say something?" She appeared in the doorway with a tray.

"I said this cool snap is giving us a reprieve."

She set the tray on the coffee table, then bent over to serve him. Her skirt hitched upward, and he wondered what she was wearing underneath.

He took the cup from her, and watched as she went to the chair farthest from him, the purple one with the gold shoes. What was there to say?

"You like gold shoes, don't you?"

"Yes. I like frivolous, gaudy, happy shoes."

Once, not too long ago, he had imagined her happy shoes lined up in his closet beside his own. Of course, that was before the bedroom fiasco.

The tea was strong and hot, just the way he liked

it. Out of the corner of his eye he watched Maxie sip hers. The way she wrapped her lips around the china cup was enticing. Every move she made enticed him.

Loss ripped through him, and for the first time since Crash's visit to his office he thought about what his brother had said. Suddenly his entire life seemed empty, and he envied his brother, envied his carefree spirit, his cocky self-confidence, his adoring wife, his fat, healthy child.

Joseph felt like a toad. What woman in her right mind would want to kiss him and turn him into a prince?

"The tea is good," he said.

"Thank you. My grandmother taught me how to make it. She said you could always tell a lady by the way she dressed and the way she made her tea. I got it only halfway right."

She sparkled when she laughed. Joseph had never noticed that about her.

"I like the way you dress." Maxie set her cup carefully on the table beside her chair and folded her hands in her lap, watching him. "You have an unconventional flair that's very appealing, Maxie."

A lovely blush colored her cheeks, and she captured him with a single glance. Mesmerized, they stared at each other. If he walked across the room and took her hand, would she lead him into her bedroom? Would she take him on that wild, frenzied ride to the stars?

His cup clattered against the tray as he set it down. Sweat trickled down the side of his face.

"Why did you come, Joe?"

Why, indeed? He wasn't sure he knew the answer.

"That's a very straightforward question. Would your grandmother approve?"

"Definitely not. But then she wouldn't approve of a lot of the things I do. I'm like my granddaddy in that way. A maverick."

If he had Crash's cocky self-assurance, he would walk across the room, lift her out of the chair, and press her against the wall. Then he'd lift that tiny skirt and bury himself in her sweet, slick folds.

"*That's* why I'm here," he would say.

If he were his brother.

"I don't like to leave unfinished business," he said.

"We have no unfinished business. Everything we started is over . . . except the christening party, and I can take care of that. All you have to do is show up and give your speech."

"This is not about the christening party." He pulled her gold shoe from a suede pouch. "I'm returning this."

"I left that in the office. Where did you get it? Did Claude give it to you?"

"This is the mate."

"How? Why?"

"Pairs belong together. How is not important."

"I don't believe this. You came all the way over here just to return my shoe."

"Not just return it." A sudden inspiration seized Joe, and he stood up before he could rationalize and change his mind. "Stay right where you are."

She sucked in her breath when he knelt in front of her chair.

"What are you doing?"

"Playing Prince Charming to your Cinderella." His grin was crooked. "I feel like a fool."

"Joe . . ." She leaned toward him, and for a moment he thought she was going to run her hands through his hair. But she pulled her hands back and sank deep into her chair. "You don't look like a fool," she whispered.

His hand trembled as he lifted her foot to his knee. He couldn't resist caressing her soft skin, tracing the tender blue veins with his fingertips.

"Please," she whispered.

"Please, what?"

"Stop before I do something we'll both regret."

She could have said anything but that, anything but *regret*. Joseph loved this woman. In spite of everything, he loved her. But he wasn't about to be the cause of her regrets.

He forced himself to smile. "If the shoe fits will you save the last dance at the christening for me?"

For a moment she closed her eyes, her lips trembling. When she opened them he thought he saw the glisten of tears.

"I'll save the last dance for you."

He bent down and kissed her instep, then slipped the shoe onto her foot. Gold sparkles winked at him, and he held on a moment longer. She let out a sigh, and he didn't dare look at her, didn't dare let her see what was in his eyes.

He left without speaking, and all the way to the door he kept hoping she would call him back. But there was nothing but silence in the room. Outside he sat behind the wheel of his Lincoln, still hoping she would rush toward the door and beckon him in. But the door remained shut.

Joseph drove straight to his office.

TWENTY-ONE

Maxie slept in the gold shoe.

The next morning when she woke up, she lurched into the kitchen on one shoe, tilting sideways, then stood at the kitchen window, looking out. The sun was shining, and three bluebirds swung on the lowest branch of the pecan tree, swooping down occasionally to hop among the daffodils.

"Bluebirds of happiness," she said.

She was so miserable, she wasn't fit company, even for herself. She called Claude and told him she was feeling under the weather, then she hopped sideways around her house, getting ready for the movies. If she had the other gold shoe, she'd wear them to the movies.

Instead she put on fuchsia high-top tennis shoes, climbed into her Beetle, and went to the saddest movie playing so she'd have plenty of reason to cry. Afterward she consoled herself with a chocolate sundae, vowing that it would be her last, that tomorrow would be another day. She sounded just like Scarlett.

Joe thought he could lose himself in work and soon his life would be back to its normal pre-Maxie state. But at night, lying in his jungle bedroom, he realized the folly of his thinking. He couldn't control love. It had happened, even when he didn't want it to, and now it wouldn't go away. No amount of rational thinking could change his heart. It had known magic, and true magic lasts forever.

At the end of a miserable week, he picked up the phone.

"Crash, I need to talk to you."

"If it's about the partnership, I've already given my answer. B. J. and I are happy with our little country practice, and we won't change our minds."

"You're right. You're where you belong, and I was an arrogant jackass to try and make you change." Jenny came over the intercom to tell him a client was waiting. "This is not about business, it's about the party. Can I drop by the house this evening to discuss it?"

"Great. I'll cook red beans and rice. Should we call and have Maxie come too? . . . Joe, are you there?"

"I'm here. I was just thinking. Do you remember that game we played as kids, the one where we were Knights of the Round Table and rode stick horses?"

"Every detail. In a few years I'll be playing that same game with my son."

"Don't call Maxie. Get out the stick horses, Crash, we're going to lay plans to storm the castle."

"Maxie, are you sitting down?"

It was B. J., calling her at the office.

"Yes." Maxie was on the sofa, sipping tea and looking at her new coffee table ornament, the pair of gold shoes Joe had rescued.

"Get this. Joseph came over last night, and he and Crash had a big secret powwow. When they emerged from the den you'd have thought both of them had received some kind of congressional award."

"B. J., does this story have a point?"

"You're certainly testy. What's wrong?"

"Chocolate overdose."

"Uh-oh, soul food. My original question stands: What's wrong?"

"Nothing that a few years won't cure." Her sister was silent, no doubt analyzing every word Maxie had said. "How did he look?"

"Who?"

"Joe."

"I thought as much."

"Nothing's going on between us, if that's what you're thinking."

"I'm sorry to hear that. In spite of the fact that both of you are as stubborn as that old mule in our barn, I think you'd be a perfect match."

"Is that why you called? To tell me I'm as stubborn as a mule?"

Claude came through the door in time to hear Maxie's comment. "I couldn't agree more," he said. "Who is that on the phone?"

She covered the mouthpiece. "It's B. J."

"Tell her I'll be at the party with bells on."

Claude could always make her smile. "Did you hear that?"

"I heard it," B. J. said. "The tent arrived this morning."

"What tent?"

"That's why I called. Didn't you and Joe order a tent for the party?"

"No. I thought it was going to be inside. Maybe Crash ordered it."

"No. He said you and Joe were taking care of everything. It's a beautiful tent, a candy-striped big top. The man who delivered it specifically said it was for baby Joe's christening party."

"Good grief."

"Oh, and there's one more thing. He said the banner would be delivered right before the party."

Maxie wasn't about to ask, "What banner?" She was beginning to feel like a parrot.

After she'd hung up, Claude sat beside her and picked up the gold shoes. "Not that I'm complaining, but do you plan to leave these here forever?"

"No, I'm going to wear them to the party." Maxie picked up the gold shoes. They were her trademark, and in a sense symbolized everything she was, uninhibited, unconventional, unsinkable. Suddenly she began to feel like her old self.

"Do you know what I was thinking, Claude?"

"No, but I hope it's wild and crazy."

"I was thinking that I might do another performance with these shoes. Who knows where they might land the next time?"

She was in bed, sans pajamas and sans chocolate, reading *War and Peace* when the phone rang.

"Hello, Maxie." Joseph's voice sent shivers all the way down to her toes.

"I hear you've erected a circus tent. Does that mean we can ditch the gray-and-white pinstriped decor?"

His roar of laughter was genuine. "Maxie, that's one of the reasons I called. I've done my part for the party. You can decorate with anything you like, with one exception."

"No zebras!" They said it simultaneously, and both of them laughed.

"I'm making no rash promises," she said. "That's one. What's the other reason you called?"

"To see if you're naked in bed. What are you wearing, Maxie?"

He was the only man she'd ever met who could seduce her merely by the tone and pitch of his voice. She had to clamp her hand over her mouth so he wouldn't hear her moan of sheer ecstasy.

"That game is over, Joseph."

"You're right. That game is over. Good night, Maxie. . . . Oh, one more thing. Don't forget to save the last dance for me."

TWENTY-TWO

They flanked Crash and B. J. and the baby, Joseph on Crash's right and Maxie on B. J.'s left. Maxie was wearing purple chiffon with gold shoes, the ones he'd returned to her. In the midst of the staid First Methodist Church, she looked like a Mardi Gras parade, and Joe couldn't take his eyes off her. She was worth having at any price.

As the minister led them and the congregation through their promises to the child, Maxie glanced at him only once, and when she caught his eye she didn't turn away for a long, breathless moment. If there was anyplace where prayers might be answered, it was the church. Joe was staking his future on today, and as he said a prayer for his nephew he also sent a petition winging heavenward for himself and for Maxie.

Claude drove with her to the farm in her little Beetle. He was in high spirits, humming snatches of songs, whistling, grinning.

"Good grief, Claude. This is a happy occasion, but aren't you overdoing it?"

"There's nothing I like better than secrets."

"What are you talking about?" She glanced at the hot pink tote bag sitting in his lap. "And what are you doing with that enormous tote? You've been wagging it around as if you're carrying the contents of Fort Knox."

"Do you think anybody at church noticed?"

"I think it's safe to say everybody who saw you, saw the bag."

He held it up and inspected it. "It is rather garish, isn't it?"

Suddenly Maxie began to laugh. "No more garish than my shoes. You never said what was in the bag."

"You'll find out soon enough."

She forgot about Claude's mysterious bag when she saw the tent. Though she'd spent all the previous day decorating, she never failed to thrill at the sight of a big top. Red-and-white striped with red flags flying from the center pole, it occupied a large portion of B. J.'s backyard. She'd strung colored balloons and streamers from every pole, and wisteria and clematis cascaded from hanging baskets, spilled from enormous urns, and flanked the pathway.

"I've hired clowns," Maxie said.

"Did you now?" Claude grinned. "I always did say,

give a man a paint box and there's no telling what he'll do."

"You're incorrigible."

"I do hope so, dear." Maxie parked the car and they stood together under a magnolia tree before going into the tent. Claude turned to give her a quick hug. "Maxie, may all your dreams come true."

"Thanks, but shouldn't that wish be for baby Joe?"

"It's a wish for all of us. . . . Do you have a handkerchief? I always get teary-eyed at celebrations."

"You're speaking to the keeper of the linen." She handed him a lace-edged hankie. "I don't know what B. J. would have done without me all these years." She was beginning to get a little teary-eyed herself. "Walk in with me, Claude."

"I wouldn't miss it for the world."

She took her friend's arm and went down the flower-bedecked pathway and into the big top. In the center ring, surrounded by ginger and orchids and all manner of exotic flowers flown in from Hawaii, stood an antique carousel. Painted wooden animals spun round and round as tiny beveled mirrors caught the enchanted faces of children.

Maxie stood dead still, her hand on her throat. "It has zebras," she said. Then, as excited as any child, she grabbed Claude's arm and dragged him across the sawdust. "Can you believe it, Claude? Painted zebras!"

"I believe it."

As she raced toward the carousel, Maxie caught a glimpse of Joseph leaning against a tent pole, looking perfectly in place wearing his tuxedo in a circus tent. A clown with huge pink shoes and a green bulbous nose helped her onto a zebra. Laughing, her head thrown back, her slender throat exposed, she rode the carousel until she was giddy.

She closed her eyes for a second, reaching out for the clown. A pair of strong arms lifted her down.

"Is it true that angels ride zebras?"

Instead of setting her on her feet, Joseph held her against his chest.

"I'm no angel."

"I could make a good case that you are."

He smelled crisp and clean, of starch and woodsy aftershave and sunshine and fresh air. Up close he looked even better than from a distance. She lolled in his arms, not caring whether he put her down or not.

"The carousel was a stroke of genius. Isn't that just like Crash to do something extravagant?"

Crash and B. J. strolled by with the baby. "Wish I could take the credit," he said, grinning. He winked at his brother and strolled on by.

"You did this?"

"Guilty."

"Baby Joe will always remember that his uncle rented a carousel for his christening party."

Joseph merely smiled, then set her on her feet. "Enjoy the party, Maxie."

Another meeting, another brush-off. She tossed her hair and stuck out her chin. "That's exactly what I intend to do."

Fuming and plotting, she marched off. Just wait till the jazz combo she hired got there. She'd show him a thing or two. If he thought her act at Bogart's was outrageous, just wait till he saw her next performance.

Crash walked to the microphone to welcome his guests to baby Joe's party, and Maxie was immediately ashamed of herself. She felt like a selfish beast, plotting her own revenge. The day belonged to baby Joe, not to her, and she was determined to make it the best christening party any little child ever had.

"None of this would have been possible without Joe's godparents," Crash was saying. "Maxie, Joe, come on up here."

They came from opposite sides of the room, but Maxie was aware of every step Joseph took. Crash joined his wife, and they were on the stage together, standing side by side at the microphone. As Maxie smiled at the crowd, Joe leaned toward her.

"Ladies and gentlemen," he whispered.

"I'm no lady and you're no gentleman."

"True, but you're the one wearing the skirt."

Maxie took her place in front of the microphone. She had tried to write a speech, but everything came out stilted and formal, so she had decided to simply speak from her heart.

"Baby Joe, you are a child created in love and welcomed into the world by adoring parents, and you already have everything you need. But your aunt Maxie has a special dream for you: I hope that you will always keep the childlike wonder that allows you to see magic."

While the crowd applauded, Joseph slid his arm around her waist and whispered, "I'm seeing magic,

Maxie." Then he was at the microphone. It had been such a brief encounter that Maxie thought she might have dreamed it. If she let herself, she could start to dream big dreams, but she'd been burned enough not to get excited by Joseph's flirtation.

"I've never been a godparent before, and I can tell you that I'm more than a little nervous." He was a man who knew how to play to a crowd. The minute they laughed, they were his. It was one more bit of evidence that he was formidable in the courtroom. He turned toward his brother with all the ease of a seasoned actor. "Next year we're swapping roles: You be the godfather up here making a fool of yourself, and I'll be the father."

Maxie turned hot and cold all at once, and she hoped her face didn't betray her turmoil. Though her heart was beating double time, she wasn't about to get her hopes up. All good litigators were good actors.

Maxie wasn't a bad actress, and she called on all her skill to stand on the stage as if nothing out of the ordinary was happening while Joseph finished his speech. As he ended there was a commotion at the tent's opening. The crowd parted, and down the pathway came a clown wearing an enormous purple wig. And behind him trotted two animals.

"Zebras," said Maxie. She looked at Joe.

"For angels," he said.

The clown stopped in front of B. J., and Crash lifted her and the baby into the saddle of the first zebra. Then the clown stopped in front of the stage.

"This one's for you, Maxie," the clown said.

"Claude?"

"Guilty."

"You knew about this."

"You didn't think I could keep a secret, did you?"

Suddenly she found herself lifted into the saddle. Joe leaned close and whispered, "Save the last dance for me, Maxie."

They rode the zebras around the big top to cheers from the crowd, then Claude brought the impromptu parade to a halt underneath a banner that read "Reserved for Angels." The band struck up "Thank Heaven for Little Girls," with the bandleader at the microphone changing the gender to little boys.

Crash led B. J. and the baby in the first dance, and Claude swept Maxie onto the floor. Joseph was nowhere in sight.

"When did you know about the zebras?" she asked.

"Only a couple of days ago. Joseph called to apologize and ask for my help."

"Apologize for what?"

"He was pretty bearish the day he discovered his bedroom suite."

Maxie groaned. "That was not one of my better impulses. I still don't know what to do about that, Claude."

"Don't worry about it. It's Joseph's house. If he wants it changed, he'll tell you."

"You're a good friend."

"So you are, Maxie."

As they swept around the dance floor, Maxie

scanned every nook and cranny for Joseph, but he seemed to have disappeared. She thought about the life she had—the loving family, the good friends, the charming house on Maxwell Street, the thriving business—and she was content.

"For two mavericks, we've done all right, haven't we, Claude?"

"Yes. In some ways we're two of a kind. You won't forget me when your prince comes to claim you, will you?"

"Never. What prince?"

"Look over your shoulder."

The song ended, and as the band began another, Claude handed Maxie over to Joseph.

"Claude deserves the first dance, but I'm selfish. I'm claiming all the rest."

"What new game is this?"

"This is no game. This is your life, and mine."

They danced just as they had loved, as if they were made for each other.

"Thank you for renting zebras, Joe."

"Do you know what they mean, Maxie?"

"If I were bold I'd say they mean you changed your mind about me."

He laughed. "You've never lacked boldness, and you would be exactly right." He pulled her closer and cradled her head against his shoulder. "I've changed my mind, but not my heart."

She tried to pull back and look up at him, but he held her fast.

"The thing I didn't know until I thought I had lost

you is this: You've always had my heart, Maxie. Always."

"Tell me the beginning."

"You love this, don't you? The romance, the grand gesture, the flowery speeches."

"As long as they come from your heart."

"They come straight from my heart, Maxie. That's a promise."

He waltzed across the sawdust and through the opening in the tent. A full moon rode across the sky, and a million stars lit the pathway. Spring flowers perfumed the air. It was a night made for romance.

Joe pulled Maxie underneath a giant magnolia, and leaning against the trunk, held her close.

"The beginning was the first time I ever saw you, Maxie. You were dressed in white, an angel, even then, though the twinkle in your eyes gave away the imp inside you. You walked into that banquet hall with your sister and I was electrified. My heart knew, even then. It just took my mind a while to catch up."

He was everything Maxie had dreamed, Mr. Perfect, saying wonderfully romantic things to her. But she had to remember that he was an expert with words. He made his living convincing people with his speeches. Was this just another level to the many games they had played, or was he playing for keeps?

She'd made too many mistakes in the past; she couldn't afford to make another. She stepped back in order to gain perspective.

"You make a convincing case, Joe."

"But you're not convinced."

"So, convince me."

Once he'd made up his mind to woo Maxie for keeps, the first part of his plan had been easy, dazzle and persuade her with all the things she loved—zebras, carousels, exotic flowers, romantic gestures—all symbols of a happy, carefree life. But it was not enough. He'd known that from the beginning. To win Maxie would take more than smoke and mirrors, more than a dazzling show under the big top.

The ring was in his pocket, a square-cut emerald surrounded by diamonds. In the midst of a spring evening with a million stars as his witness, Joseph Patrick Beauregard dropped to his knees.

"I love you, Maxine Elizabeth Corban . . ."

Her smile was one of pure delight. "How did you know my name?"

"Magic." He took the ring from its box, and it looked like stars caught in the palm of his hand. "I don't know everything there is to know about you, but I want to know. I want to spend the rest of my life solving the delightful puzzle of Maxie. Will you marry me?"

"This means forever, doesn't it?"

"Yes. This means forever. What will your answer be, Magic Maxie?"

Her grin was impish. "My answer will be yes, on one condition."

"Is this negotiable?"

"No."

"Then tell me the condition."

"That I get to see that mole on your left hip. The

other night in your wild-animal kingdom, I was too busy to look."

He slid the ring on her finger, then picked her up and spun her around. Inside the big top the band struck up "Hard Hearted Hannah"—the vamp of Savannah.

"They're playing our song, Maxie."

"You did that, too, didn't you?"

"Yes."

She rained kisses over his face. "Joseph Patrick Beauregard, I love you to pieces."

He stood very still, and when she pressed her lips against his, he kissed her for a very long time.

"This is the last dance, Maxie."

"I saved it for you."

He slid her to her feet, and they spun among the flowers.

"You know where the last dance leads, don't you?" he whispered.

"Yes. Take me there."

He'd left soft lights burning in his bedroom, and now he added candles, dozens of them, flickering like fireflies in a jungle.

"Stand right where you are, Maxie."

Joseph knelt, took off her gold shoes, and kissed each toe. Then he put the shoes on a shelf he'd added to the wall beside the bed.

"My trophy. What do you think, Maxie?"

"It adds the right touch if you want to be daring and different."

He laughed with sheer joy. With Maxie he would always be challenged, always be surprised. He stalked her, eyes glowing.

"Do you want to take off my pants and let me show you just how daring and different I can be?"

"How can I resist?"

It was her turn to kneel. His zipper made a soft click in the stillness.

"Do I have to take them off right away?" Her hand was on him, doing magical things. And then her mouth.

He was filled with such a wildness and sense of freedom that he wanted to race into the streets and shout it to the rooftops.

She slid his pants to the floor, then gave a whoop of joy.

"Leopard print," she said.

"Jockeys, size thirty-four." He wrapped his arms around her waist and backed her against the wall. "The jungle beast is hungry, Maxie. Feel him roar."

Her skirts billowed over his head as he took his fill. Soon that was not enough, he had to have more. He wrapped her legs around his waist. Their wild, primitive dance sent them reeling against the walls and tumbling over the floor.

"You are incredible," he said.

"Only with you, my love, only with you."

He peeled her dress away, and his clothes fell in a

heap on hers. The mattress sagged under their weight, and when she was spread upon his bed, lush and dewy and sensual, he made slow, exquisite love to her, to his magic Maxie, his dream, his love.

There was nothing simple about the way they loved, nothing predictable or ordinary. Each touch thrilled, each thrust electrified, each kiss transported them to that realm where only true lovers go, that shining place beyond the stars.

And when at last they lay in each other's arms, sated, Maxie brushed his hair tenderly back from his forehead.

"I was so busy I forgot to see your mole."

"I love the way you stay busy, Maxie. Do you always stay busy like that?"

"That depends on who I'm with."

"Minx. There's only one person you'll be with from now on and that's me."

"In that case . . . indeed, counselor, I plan to stay busy like that for the rest of my life."

"Hmmm." He closed his eyes and pretended to be asleep.

"Roll over, Joe."

He laughed, loving this playful side of her. "Now? Just when I was getting comfortable."

"Right this very minute."

He turned on his stomach, and she leaned close to inspect his left hip.

"This is incredible," she said. "I don't believe it." She traced his mole with the tips of her fingers. Shivers went all over him. "A lion! Are you sure this is real?"

"It's real, all right, Maxie. And it's already roaring again." He flipped over and pulled her down on top of him. Smiling, she began to rock and sway above him.

"I've never refused to answer the call of the wild."

EPILOGUE

Nine months later

B. J. and Crash rushed down the corridor of the hospital toward room 413, carrying a huge stuffed animal.

"I've never carried a zebra's tail before," he said. "Want to swap ends?"

"Hush up and hang on to your end. Humility becomes you, my love."

A huge bouquet of balloons adorned the door, and from inside drifted the sound of a tape, playing softly. B. J. and Crash stood outside, shifting the gigantic stuffed zebra into an upright position.

"Great Caesar's pony cart. Is that song what I think it is?"

B. J. grinned at her husband. "What did you expect. They even played it at their wedding, remember?"

"How could I forget? Joe set Maxie on top of the table right by the wedding cake and she belted it out.

That was the sexiest rendition of "Hard Hearted Hannah" I ever heard."

"The best part was when she tossed those gold shoes at Joe, and he served up the champagne in them."

"No," he said softly. "The best part is waiting beyond this door."

Crash pushed it open, then wrapped his arm around his wife as memories washed over him. There was his brother, bending over the bed, and there was his brother's wife, her red hair like flame on the pillow, gazing up at her husband with adoring eyes, a baby cradled against each breast.

"Twins," Maxie said. "Can you believe it?"

"Of course I can." B. J. handed the little girl to Crash and cradled the little boy in her arms. "You never did anything halfway in your life."

"She certainly doesn't." Joe kissed his wife in the way of a man deeply in love, then sat on the edge of the bed, holding her hand. "I guess you two know what this means."

B. J. pretended surprise. "Surely you're not going to ask us to be the godparents."

"Of course he is," Crash said. "Remember what he said at Joey's christening party. Joseph always keeps his promises."

"He certainly does." Maxie caressed her husband's face.

Just then the door burst open, and in came Claude, carrying another enormous stuffed zebra. He set the zebra beside the one B. J. and Crash had brought, then took both babies in his arms.

"Well, I guess you two little darlings expect old Uncle Claude to get out his clown suit and do that live zebra bit all over again, don't you?"

"Of course they do," the babies' parents and aunt and uncle chorused.

Claude blustered and carried on, but his chest was puffed out with pride.

"Do you have any idea how mean those little devils can be? One of them kept trying to bite me on the butt and the other left an odious trail. If I hadn't done some fancy footwork, my clown shoes would be ruined." He kissed each baby on the forehead. "Now you two little rascals expect me to do all that again?"

"No one but you could possibly do it, Claude." Maxie reached for his hand. He placed the babies in her arms, then sat on the opposite side of the bed, holding her hand.

"Anything for Magic Maxie," he said.

Later, when the guests had gone and the babies were tucked into their cribs fast asleep, Joe bent over his wife.

"Anything for my magic Maxie," he whispered.

"Is the lion roaring?" she said.

He pulled her close and buried his face in her hair. "Always, my love. Always."

THE EDITORS' CORNER

Everybody has a classic story that has endured in their heart through the years. There's always that one story that makes you think *What if . . . ?* This month we present four new LOVESWEPTs, each based on a treasured tale of the past, with their own little twists of fate. It is said that differences keep people apart, but we've found the opposite to be true. Differences make life interesting, adding zest and spice to our lives. We hope you'll enjoy exploring those differences in opinion, station, and attitude that ensure a happy ending for our LOVESWEPT characters this month.

In Pat Van Wie's **ROUGH AROUND THE EDGES,** LOVESWEPT #870, Kristen Helton is about to meet her match in one doozy of a hero, Alex Jamison. Alex grew up on the streets of Miami and now he's devoted his life to keeping the local community center open. But when Kristen insists on joining his fight to keep kids out of trouble, Alex has to accept that he may have been wrong about the gorgeous young doctor. The tensions run high after Alex decides to sacrifice himself to raise money for the center. Kristen discovers his secret and comes to realize that maybe their worlds aren't so different after all. In the true tradition of Robin Hood, Pat Van Wie delights as she shows us how we must persevere against all odds.

Maureen Caudill is giving Jason Cooper his comeuppance in **NEVER SAY GOOD-BYE**, LOVESWEPT #871. When last seen, Jason was playing the part of die-hard bachelor scoffing at his sister and best friend's domestic bliss in DADDY CANDIDATE, LOVESWEPT #797. Years later, C. J. Stone's magazine names Jason the Sexiest Businessman in California. Now Jason is desperate to get C.J. off his back and believes that a nerdy facade will make her change her mind about him. C.J. and Jason seem to disagree about everything. Even watching *It's a Wonderful Life* causes a clash of beliefs between them. But the one thing they can't argue about is their growing attraction to each other—it's undeniable. With humor and grace, Maureen Caudill plots a collision course for these mismatched lovers.

Stephanie Bancroft retells the story of Aladdin in **YOUR WISH IS MY COMMAND,** LOVE-SWEPT #872. "I shall grant you three of your heart's desires" is the last thing Ladden Sanderson expects to hear after an earthquake reduces his antiques store to a shambles. Jasmine Crowne doesn't understand why now, after three years of friendship, she suddenly longs to feel Ladden's arms around her. And no one can explain the strange man who keeps muttering something about wishes—or the antique carpet Ladden is reserving for Jasmine that keeps popping up in the weirdest places. Can a benevolent genie help this quiet diamond in the rough win over the woman he's always loved? Stephanie Bancroft charms readers as she weaves a delectable romance liberally spiced with marvelous miracles and fantasy.

Five years ago Liam Bartlett was saved from a San Salustiano prison with the help of young freedom fighter Marisala Bolivar. Now Mara is all grown up and both are about to learn **FREEDOM'S PRICE**, LOVESWEPT #873, by Suzanne Brockmann. When Mara's uncle sends her to Boston to get an education and, unbeknownst to her, learn to be a proper lady, he asks his friend Liam to take care of her, to be her guardian. Liam finds it harder and harder to see Mara as the young girl she once was, but his promise to her uncle stands in his way. Mara has loved Liam forever, and she does her best to get him to see her as the woman she has become. Suzanne Brockmann seals the fate of two lovers as they learn to battle the past and look to the future.

Happy reading!

With warmest wishes,

Susann Brailey

Joy Abella

Susann Brailey
Senior Editor

Joy Abella
Administrative Editor

P.S. Watch for these Bantam women's fiction titles coming in January! Hailed as "an accomplished story-teller" by the *Los Angeles Daily News*, nationally best-selling author Jane Feather concludes her charm bracelet trilogy with **THE EMERALD SWAN.** An exquisite emerald charm sets in motion a tale of suspense, laughter, and love, and brings together twin girls separated on a night of terror. Newcomer Shana Abé delivers **A ROSE IN WINTER.** In the year 1280, a time of dark turbulence, Solange is forced to scorn her greatest love in order to protect him, an act that leaves her imprisoned in the terrifying reaches of hell until Damon becomes her unwitting rescuer. From *New York Times* bestselling author Iris Johansen comes a new hardcover novel of suspense, **AND THEN YOU DIE. . . .** Photojournalist Bess Grady witnesses a nightmarish experiment conducted by international conspirators. With the help of a mysterious agent, Bess escapes their clutches, vowing to do whatever it takes to stop them from succeeding in their deadly plan. And immediately following this page, preview the Bantam women's fiction titles on sale in December!

For current information on Bantam's women's fiction, visit our new Web site, *Isn't It Romantic*, at the following address:

http://www.bdd.com/romance

Don't miss these extraordinary books
by your favorite Bantam authors!

On sale in December:

THE PERFECT HUSBAND
by Lisa Gardner

STARCATCHER
by Patricia Potter

THE PERFECT HUSBAND

by Lisa Gardner

*Jim Beckett was everything she'd ever dreamed of. But two
years after Tess married the decorated cop and bore his
child, she helped put him behind bars for savagely murder-
ing ten women. Even locked up in a maximum security
prison, he vowed he would come after her and make her
pay. Now the cunning killer has escaped—and the most
dangerous game of all begins. . . .*

*After a lifetime of fear, Tess will do something she's
never done before. She's going to learn to protect her
daughter and fight back, with the help of a burned-out ex-
marine. As the largest manhunt four states have ever seen
mobilizes to catch Beckett, the clock winds down to the terrifying reunion between husband and wife. And Tess knows
that this time, her only choices are to kill—or be killed.*

Tess Williams awoke as she'd learned to awaken—
slowly, degree by degree, so that she reached con-
sciousness without ever giving herself away. First her
ears woke up, seeking out the sound of another person breathing. Next, her skin prickled to life, searching for the burning length of her husband's body
pressed against her back. Finally, when her ears registered no sound and her skin found her alone in her
bed, her eyes opened, going automatically to the

closet and checking the small wooden chair she'd jammed beneath the doorknob in the middle of the night.

The chair was still in place. She released the breath she'd been holding and sat up. The empty room was already bright with mid-morning sun, the adobe walls golden and cheery. The air was hot. Her T-shirt stuck to her back, but maybe the sweat came from nightmares that never quite went away. She'd once liked mornings. They were difficult for her now, but not as difficult as night, when she would lie there and try to force her eyes to give up their vigilant search of shadows in favor of sleep.

You made it, she told herself. *You actually made it.*

For the last two years she'd been running, clutching her four-year-old daughter's hand and trying to convince Samantha that everything would be all right. She'd picked up aliases like decorative accessories and new addresses like spare parts. But she'd never really escaped. Late at night, she would sit at the edge of her daughter's bed, stroking Samantha's golden hair, and stare at the closet with fatalistic eyes.

She knew just what kind of monsters hid in the closet. She had seen the crime scene photos of what they could do. Three weeks ago, her personal monster had broken out of a maximum security prison by beating two guards to death in under sixty seconds.

Tess had called Lieutenant Lance Difford. He'd called Vince. The wheels were set in motion. Tess Williams had hidden Samantha safely away, then she had traveled as far as she could travel. Then she had traveled some more.

First, she'd taken the train, and the train had taken her through New England fields of waving grass and industrial sectors of twisted metal. Then she'd caught a plane, flying over everything as if that would help her forget and covering so many miles she left behind even fall and returned to summer.

Landing in Phoenix was like arriving in a moon crater: everything was red, dusty, and bordered by distant blue mountains. She'd never seen palms; here roads were lined with them. She'd never seen cactus; here they covered the land like an encroaching army.

The bus had only moved her farther into alien terrain. The red hills had disappeared, the sun had gained fury. Signs for cities had been replaced by signs reading STATE PRISON IN AREA. DO NOT STOP FOR HITCHHIKERS.

The reds and browns had seeped away until the bus rolled through sun-baked amber and bleached-out greens. The mountains no longer followed like kindly grandfathers. In this strange, harsh land of southern Arizona, even the hills were tormented, flayed alive methodically by mining trucks and bull-dozers.

It was the kind of land where you really did expect to turn and see the OK Corral. The kind of land where lizards were beautiful and coyotes cute. The kind of land where the hothouse rose died and the prickly cactus lived.

It was perfect.

Tess climbed out of bed. She moved slowly. Her right leg was stiff and achy, the jagged scar twitching with ghost pains. Her left wrist throbbed, ringed by a harsh circle of purple bruises. She could tell it wasn't anything serious—her father had taught her a lot about broken bones. As things went in her life these days, a bruised wrist was the least of her concerns.

She turned her attention to the bed.

She made it without thinking, tucking the corners

tightly and smoothing the covers with military precision.

I want to be able to bounce a quarter off that bed, Theresa. Youth is no excuse for sloppiness. You must always seek to improve.

She caught herself folding back the edge of the sheet over the light blanket and dug her fingertips into her palms. In a deliberate motion, she ripped off the blanket and dumped it on the floor.

"I will not make the bed this morning," she stated to the empty room. "I choose not to make the bed."

She wouldn't clean anymore either, or wash dishes or scrub floors. She remembered too well the scent of ammonia as she rubbed down the windows, the doorknobs, the banisters. She'd found the pungent odor friendly, a deep-clean sort of scent.

This is my house, and not only does it look clean, but it smells clean.

Later, Lieutenant Difford had explained to her how ammonia was one of the few substances that rid surfaces of fingerprints.

Now she couldn't smell ammonia without feeling ill.

Her gaze was drawn back to the bed, the rumpled sheets, the covers tossed and wilted on the floor. For a moment, the impulse, the sheer *need* to make that bed—and make it right because she had to seek to improve herself, you should always seek to improve—nearly overwhelmed her. Sweat beaded her upper lip. She fisted her hands to keep them from picking up the blankets.

"Don't give in. He messed with your mind, Tess, but that's done now. You belong to yourself and you are tough. You won, dammit. You *won*."

The words didn't soothe her. She crossed to the

bureau to retrieve her gun from her purse. Only at the last minute did she remember that the .22 had fallen on the patio.

J.T. Dillon had it now.

She froze. She had to have her gun. She ate with her gun, slept with her gun, walked with her gun. She couldn't be weaponless. *Defenseless, vulnerable, weak.*

Oh God. Her breathing accelerated, her stomach plummeted, and her head began to spin. She walked the edge of the anxiety attack, feeling the shakes and knowing that she either found solid footing now or lunged into the abyss.

Breathe, Tess, breathe. But the friendly desert air kept flirting with her lungs. She bent down and forcefully caught a gulp by her knees, squeezing her eyes shut.

"Can I walk you home?"

She was startled. "You mean me?" She hugged her school books more tightly against her Mt. Greylock High sweater. She couldn't believe the police officer was addressing her. She was not the sort of girl handsome young men addressed.

"No," he teased lightly. "I'm talking to the grass." He pushed himself away from the tree, his smile unfurling to reveal two charming dimples. All the girls in her class talked of those dimples, dreamed of those dimples. "You're Theresa Matthews, right?"

She nodded stupidly. She should move. She knew she should move. She was already running late for the store and her father did not tolerate tardiness.

She remained standing there, staring at this young man's handsome face. He looked so strong. A man of the law. A man of integrity? For one moment she found herself thinking, If I told you everything, would you save me? Would somebody please save me?

"*Well, Theresa Matthews, I'm Officer Beckett. Jim Beckett.*"

"*I know.*" Her gaze fell to the grass. "*Everyone knows who you are.*"

"*May I walk you home, Theresa Matthews? Would you allow me the privilege?*"

She remained uncertain, too overwhelmed to speak. Her father would kill her. Only promiscuous young women, evil women, enticed men to walk them home. But she didn't want to send Jim Beckett away. She didn't know what to do.

He leaned over and winked at her. His blue eyes were so clear, so calm. So steady.

"*Come on, Theresa, I'm a cop. If you can't trust me, who can you trust?*"

"I won," she muttered by her knees. "Dammit, I won!"

But she wanted to cry. She'd won, but the victory remained hollow, the price too high. He'd done things to her that never should have been done. He'd taken things from her that she couldn't afford to lose. Even now, he was still in her head.

Someday soon, he would kill her. He'd promised to cut out her still-beating heart, and Jim always did what he said.

She forced her head up. She took a deep breath. She pressed her fists against her thighs. "Fight, Tess. It's all you have left."

She pushed away from the dresser and moved to her suitcase, politely brought to her room by Freddie. She'd made it here, step one of her plan. Next, she had to get J.T. to agree to train her. Dimly, she remembered mentioning her daughter to him. That had been a mistake. Never tell them more than you have to, never tell the truth if a lie will suffice.

Maybe J.T. wouldn't remember. He hadn't seemed too sober. Vincent should've warned her about his drinking.

She didn't know much about J.T. Vince had said J.T. was the kind of man who could do anything he wanted to, but who didn't seem to want to do much. He'd been raised in a wealthy, well-connected family in Virginia, attended West Point, but then left for reasons unknown and joined the Marines. Then he'd left the Marines and struck out solo, rapidly earning a reputation for a fearlessness bordering on insanity. As a mercenary, he'd drifted toward doing the impossible and been indifferent to anything less. He hated politics, loved women. He was fanatical about fulfilling his word and noncommittal about everything else.

Five years ago, he'd up and left the mercenary business without explanation. Like the prodigal son, he'd returned to Virginia and in a sudden flurry of unfathomable activity, he'd married, adopted a child, and settled down in the suburbs as if all along he'd really been a shoe salesman. Later, a sixteen-year-old with a new Camaro and even newer license had killed J.T.'s wife and son in a head-on collision.

And J.T. had disappeared in Arizona.

She hadn't expected him to be drinking. She hadn't expected him to still appear so strong. She'd pictured him as being older, maybe soft and overripe around the middle, a man who'd once been in his prime but now was melting around the edges. Instead, he'd smelled of tequila. His body had been toned and hard. He'd moved fast, pinning her without any effort. He had black hair, covering his head, his arms, his chest.

Jim had had no hair, not on his head, not on his body. He'd been completely hairless, smooth as marble. Like a swimmer, she'd thought, and only later understood the full depth of her naiveté. Jim's touch had always been cold and dry, as if he was too perfect for such things as sweat. The first time she'd heard him urinate, she'd felt a vague sense of surprise; he gave the impression of being above such basic biological functions.

Jim had been perfect. Mannequin perfect. If only she'd held that thought longer.

She'd stick with J.T. Dillon. He'd once saved orphans. He'd been married and had a child. He'd destroyed things for money. He sounded skilled, he appeared dangerous.

For her purposes, he would do.

And if helping her cost J.T. Dillon too much?

She already knew the answer, she'd spent years coming to terms with it.

Sometimes, she did wish she was sixteen again. She'd been a normal girl, once. She'd dreamed of a white knight who would rescue her. Someone who would never hit her. Someone who would hold her close and tell her she was finally safe.

Now, she remembered the feel of her finger tightening around the trigger. The pull of the trigger, the jerk of the trigger, the roar of the gun and the ringing in her ears.

The acrid smell of gunpowder and the hoarse sound of Jim's cry. The thud of his body falling down. The raw scent of fresh blood pooling on her carpet.

She remembered these things.

And she knew she could do anything.

From award-winning author Patricia Potter comes a spectacular novel set in the wild Scottish Highlands, where a daring beauty and a fearless lord defy treachery and danger to find their heart's destiny . . .

STARCATCHER
by Patricia Potter

Marsali Gunn had been betrothed to Patrick Sutherland when she was just a girl, yet even then she knew the handsome warrior would have no rival in her heart or her dreams. But when Patrick returns from distant battlefields, a bitter feud has shattered the alliance between clans, and Marsali prepares to wed another chieftain. Boldly, Patrick steals what is rightfully his, damning the consequences. And Marsali is forced to make a choice: between loyalty to her people or a still-burning love that could plunge her and Patrick into the center of a deadly war . . .

"Patricia Potter has a special gift for giving an audience a first-class romantic story line."
—*Affaire de Coeur*

"One of the romance genre's finest talents."
—*Romantic Times*

He had dreamed of her. It was so much more than she'd ever expected. Her legs trembled as his tongue touched her lips, then slipped inside her mouth. A wave of new sensations rushed through her. Yet she did nothing to discourage the intimate way he explored her. Instead, she found herself responding to his every touch.

Somehow, with what was left of her wits, she realized she was clinging to him, as if her life were forfeit. She heard the small, throaty sounds she was making. She felt his entire body shaking, and she felt the hard, vital evidence of his manhood pressed against her. She had heard servants talk; she knew where this was leading. And she wanted it, wanted to move even closer to him, to join her body intimately with his.

But she could not build her own happiness on the blood of others, especially not the blood of her kin and the kin of the man she loved.

She had to return to Abernie. She had to go through with the wedding. . . .

Tearing herself from Patrick's embrace, Marsali let out a pained, hopeless cry. Surprised, Patrick let her go, his arms dropping to his sides. His breathing was ragged as his eyes questioned her.

"I canna," she said brokenly.

"We were pledged," he replied, his voice hoarse. "You are mine, Marsali."

The note of possessiveness in his voice, even given the feelings he aroused in her, stunned her. The flat, almost emotionless tone was so authoritative, so . . . certain. He'd become a stranger again, one who made decisions without consulting her.

"Our betrothal was broken," she said quietly, "cried off by both families."

"Not by me," he said.

She studied him obliquely. "My father and Edward . . . they will go after your family," she said.

"They will *try*." Coldness underlined his voice.

"Your father killed my aunt," she said desperately.

"Nay, my father is as puzzled by her disappearance as any man, and, despite his faults, he does not lie."

"Not even with death as a consequence?"

"Not even then."

Lifting her chin a notch, Marsali continued. "He accused my aunt of adultery."

"He says there was proof," Patrick replied.

His eyes glittered with the hardness of stone, and she glimpsed what his enemies must have seen of Patrick Sutherland. The thought of him at war with her father and brother made her shiver.

Dear Mother in heaven. The wedding should have started by now. Everyone would be looking for the bride. When would they begin to suspect the Sutherlands?

"I have to return to Abernie," she whispered.

"Jeanie said she would not help us if she wasn't sure you didna want the wedding," Patrick said flatly. "Was she wrong, lass? Do you want to wed Sinclair?"

"Aye," Marsali said defiantly, even though she was certain the lie must be plain on her face.

"Because of your sister?" Patrick guessed.

"Because you and I can never be."

He studied her for a moment, then, slowly, the tension left his face. He lifted his hand to trail a finger along her cheek. "You have become a beautiful woman," he said quietly. "But then, I always knew you would."

Her resolve melted under the words, under the intensity of his gaze, under the force of his demand for the truth. She leaned into his touch, craving it.

His hands were strong, she thought, from years of wielding a sword. But she could well destroy him, as well as both of their families, if she did not return.

"I *agreed* to the marriage with Edward," she said as firmly as she could. "I gave him my troth."

His hand trailed downward over her shoulder, her arm, until he took her hand in his. He squeezed her fingers, saying, "You had already given it to me with your words and, a minute ago, you gave it to me with your body. Your heart is mine, Marsali."

"And *your* heart?" she asked.

A muscle flexed in his throat, but he said nothing, and she wondered for a moment whether he had come for her out of affection—or simply because she was a belonging he wasn't ready to forfeit.

She pulled away and turned to gaze at the rocks, the hills, anything but the face made even more attractive to her by the character the years had given it. "Where would we go?"

"To Brinaire," he said flatly.

"And Cecilia?"

"Aye, she will come with us. You will both be safe there."

"Your father? He agrees?"

He hesitated long enough that she knew the answer.

"He will have to," he said. "Or we will go to France. I have friends there."

She turned and looked at him again. "And then our clans will fight one another. Many will die or starve because of us. Can you live with that?"

His mouth twisted. "They seem destined to fight now in any event."

"But there has been naught but a few minor raids," she said. "If I were to go with you, my father would not be satisfied with anything but blood. His pride—"

"Damn his pride!" Patrick burst out. "I canna

stand aside and see you marry Sinclair. The man is a coward. And his wife's death was more than a little odd."

When she only stared at him, saying nothing, he sighed heavily and shoved his fingers through his thick, black hair. Her gaze followed the gesture, falling on the scar on his wrist that he'd gotten saving her ferret's life so many years ago. Reaching out, she took Patrick's hand in hers, her fingers touching the rough, white mark from the hawk's talons. Its jagged length ran from the first knuckle of his fourth finger down his forearm to four inches past his wrist.

"Will you make an oath to me, Patrick Sutherland?" she asked, lifting her gaze to meet his.

"Aye," he said, nodding slowly. "Anything but return you to Sinclair."

"Send my sister away. Send her someplace safe. I know only my father's friends."

His gaze bore into hers. "I do know someone. Rufus's family. I was wounded, and they cared for me. There are five sisters, as well as Rufus and an older brother and his wife. It is as fine a family as I've ever known—and as generous a one. They live in an old keep in the Lowlands and socialize very little, though they bear a fine name. Their clan is very loyal to them."

"Will you see her safely there? Do you swear? No matter what happens between you and me?" She heard the desperation in her voice and saw, by the fierce glitter in his eyes, that he'd heard it, too.

"I swear it, lass," he said.

"Thank you." Marsali closed her eyes briefly.

She didn't resist when he took her in his arms again, pulling her gently toward him. She leaned against him, listening to the beating of his heart, the fine strong rhythm of it, and savoring the warmth of his body.

For a long minute, she huddled within his embrace, trying not to think of Abernie Castle, trying not to imagine the worry everyone—everyone but Jeanie—must be feeling by now. Shortly, when a search of the castle didn't turn up either her or Cecilia, panic would seize them. The two daughters of the keep gone without a trace.

She had to return. Still, she would not be returning the same person as she was when she left. Fear had turned into hope, if not happiness. Patrick had given her the means to refuse the marriage to Edward Sinclair. As long as she knew Cecilia was safe, no one would be able to force the words from her mouth. And by refusing marriage with Sinclair, she would break the alliance that would have crushed Patrick's family. Her father could not attack the Sutherlands on his own. Perhaps a war could be prevented, after all.

She would make her father believe that no Sutherland was involved in her sister's disappearance. Only herself. He would be furious. But he could do little.

Her heart would never be whole again. She could already feel it breaking, shattering into tiny shards of pain. But she would have the comfort of knowing she had prevented bloodshed.

She only wished that, one day, her father—and brother—might understand what she had given up.

On sale in January:

*AND THEN
YOU DIE . . .*
by Iris Johansen

*THE EMERALD
SWAN*
by Jane Feather

*A ROSE
IN WINTER*
by Shana Abé

DON'T MISS THESE FABULOUS
BANTAM WOMEN'S FICTION TITLES

On Sale in January
AND THEN YOU DIE...
by IRIS JOHANSEN
the New York Times *bestselling author of* THE UGLY DUCKLING

When an American photojournalist stumbles into a sinister plot designed to spread terror and destruction, she will do anything—risk everything—to save her family and untold thousands of innocent lives.

_____ 10616-3 $22.95/$29.95

THE EMERALD SWAN
by the incomparable JANE FEATHER,
nationally bestselling author of VICE *and* VANITY

A major bestselling force whom the *Los Angeles Daily News* calls "an accomplished storyteller," Jane Feather pens the much anticipated third book in her "Charm Bracelet" trilogy: the mesmerizing tale of twin girls who grow up as strangers—and the dark and magnetic Earl who holds the key to their destinies.

_____ 57525-2 $5.99/$7.99

A ROSE IN WINTER
from the exciting new voice of SHANA ABÉ

Brimming with passion and intrigue, enchantment and alchemy, England is brought to life in its most turbulent time, as two lovers risk political exile and certain death to keep their love in bloom.

_____ 57787-5 $5.50/$7.50

Ask for these books at your local bookstore or use this page to order.

Please send me the books I have checked above. I am enclosing $_____ (add $2.50 to cover postage and handling). Send check or money order, no cash or C.O.D.'s, please.

Name _____

Address _____

City/State/Zip _____

Send order to: Bantam Books, Dept. FN159, 2451 S. Wolf Rd., Des Plaines, IL 60018.
Allow four to six weeks for delivery.
Prices and availability subject to change without notice.   FN 158 1/98